THE FROGRATS

Joe Hartwell

MINERVA PRESS
LONDON
MONTREUX   LOS ANGELES   SYDNEY

THE FROGRATS
Copyright © Joe Hartwell 1997

All Rights Reserved

No part of this book may be reproduced in any form,
by photocopying or by any electronic or mechanical means,
including information storage or retrieval systems,
without permission in writing from both the copyright owner
and the publisher of this book.

ISBN 1 86106 356 3

First Published 1997 by
MINERVA PRESS
195 Knightsbridge,
London SW7 1RE.

Printed in Great Britain by
Arrowhead Books Ltd, Reading, Berkshire

THE FROGRATS

Acknowledgements

Firstly, I would like to thank my two young daughters: Sabrina for telling me all about the poisonous tree frogs which gave me part of the idea for writing *The Frograts*; and Stephanie, whose words one day, "Ah, that's my Daddy," meant more to me than she will ever realise.

Secondly, to Sheila Holligon (author of *Nightrider* and *Bridestone*) whose enthusiastic encouragement I found to be invaluable.

Thirdly, to all my family and my friends, but especially those who gave me the necessary inspiration and motivation for my first two novels; *The Frograts* and *The Mist*. These, I hope, will be the first of many.

Last but not least. To my ex-wife. Folks, she put up with more than any wife has ever had to put up with. I am happy to say we are still friends.

I love you all.

Joe Hartwell.

About the Author

Joe Hartwell was born in Hertfordshire in 1959. He is from a deeply religious background and was brought up strictly with high moral standards, so some of the content of his first two novels, *The Frograts* and *The Mist*, has surprised many of his closest friends.

He was a constable in the Bedfordshire Police but resigned as a protest against soft sentencing, and still feels that Criminals' Rights are a rude gesture in the direction of the victims. The darker side of human nature is borne out vividly in his first two novels, but he hopes that they might symbolise wrong-doers getting their just deserts in the end.

He is currently working on a third novel which is horror/dark fantasy.

Contents

Prologue	9
Chapter One	11
Chapter Two	15
Chapter Three	24
Chapter Four	32
Chapter Five	37
Chapter Six	47
Chapter Seven	53
Chapter Eight	65
Chapter Nine	72
Chapter Ten	77
Chapter Eleven	82
Chapter Twelve	88
Chapter Thirteen	92
Chapter Fourteen	102
Chapter Fifteen	107
Chapter Sixteen	117
Chapter Seventeen	128

Chapter Eighteen	141
Chapter Nineteen	153
Chapter Twenty	166
Chapter Twenty-One	176
Chapter Twenty-Two	184
Epilogue	190
Epilogue Part Two	191

Prologue

Beneath the old, rotten fence which had been knocked flat during a storm over a year ago, by the rundown farmhouse, in the overgrown, neglected garden, lurked two hideous living things. One of them in some ways resembled a large, fat mouse. It had a long, thin tail and its body was certainly shaped like a mouse and was covered in white, bristly hair. That, however, was where its similarity with a mouse ended, for above its obese shoulders there was something incredibly unusual about it - not just for a mouse, but for any of God's creations.

It had been in darkness for so long that it was virtually blind, but it had instinctively chewed and scratched at its surroundings until, after a while, it had been able to move. Suddenly it had sensed freedom, although still aware of many other creatures of its own kind around it. Its instincts had told it to keep on moving, and the other creatures, all except one, ignored it and let it go.

It had found safety and shelter. The old, rotten fence offered it these comforts, but its tiny brain gradually became aware of another problem.

Hunger.

The other loathsome, living object, the one that had faithfully followed it, still crouched next to it. It peered through the tunnel which led out from the garden, but this one resembled not a mouse, but, more closely, a frog which was quite small and had curious yellow flecks on its clammy skin.

And this second creature possessed the twitching snout of a rat. It sat there as an obscene insult to nature, but with its small brain, unaware of how it had come to be there at all, it continued to peer up the tunnel, with horrid drool glistening on its pointed rat's teeth. It appeared to be grinning.

Chapter One

Brian Austin made himself comfortable in his usual spot by the river, then took a leisurely look along the path in both directions. He wanted to confirm that he was in the best position to see anyone coming along, but because of the thick foliage any pedestrians would not be able to see him unless they came searching. At fourteen, he should have been at school, but he couldn't be bothered. Once a week, with games and maths to look forward to, he treated himself to the afternoon off.

He got out his packet of cigarettes, lit one, took a deep drag and then exhaled and watched the smoke drift away with the wind. 'Lovely fags,' he thought. People went on about how bad they were for your health, but he knew how many he could smoke. He laughed to himself, took another drag and coughed.

This was the fourth Friday afternoon on the trot that he had come down to this place. He was getting to be a dab hand at forging his mother's signature. He'd simply spotted the place one Saturday morning when out with his dog, typed out a note on the word processor at school, then endorsed it with a forged signature. He did not know how long he would be able to get away with it, but he was sure the idea still had some mileage left in it.

Just as he was taking another puff of his cigarette, a movement caught his eye from the edge of the river only a few yards away. At first he thought he had imagined it, because as he concentrated on the spot he saw nothing except green and yellow plants.

Then he saw the creature hop. Green and yellow, it was the same colour as the plants, and the second he realised that it was a frog, it suddenly hopped up into a tree.

"Bloody hell!" he whispered to himself. He had never seen a frog do that before.

He tossed away his half-smoked cigarette, then jogged over to where the frog was still sitting, a few feet up into the tree. Close up he could clearly see strange orange markings on it. He had never seen a frog like it before.

He laughed at it, and reached out to touch it.

It opened its mouth and croaked. He laughed again, deciding that he would take it home and keep it as a pet.

It opened its mouth again, but this time squirted a stream of clear liquid into his face. Some went into his eyes, stinging him and temporarily blinding him. Some went into his mouth. It was like hot, bitter acid.

He spat onto the ground and rubbed his eyes, but by the time he was able to see again, the frog had vanished.

It was at about six o'clock that evening when Mr and Mrs Austin and their two boys sat down to their evening meal. Brian was suffering from a severe headache and was eating very slowly.

His mother, for the third time, looked at him anxiously. "Are you all right, Brian?" she said quietly.

"Of course," he said gruffly. "Why shouldn't I be?"

"Now don't talk to your mother like that!" his father told him. "Point is, you do look a bit off colour."

Brian banged his fork down on the table.

"I am okay," he shouted. "Okay?"

"I know what's wrong," said Ben, his ten-year-old brother. "He bunked off from school again, and..."

"I'm warning you," Brian told him, pointing his knife at him. "Shut up!"

"What did you say?" Mr Austin asked Ben.

"He's done it before," Ben grinned, "but this time, he..."

"One last chance," Brian hissed. "You say another word and I'll..."

"Brian!" Mrs Austin gasped, shocked at her elder son's sudden anger and hatred towards young Ben.

But Brian ignored her and continued his remarks to his younger brother. "You tell and *I'll kill you*."

"Brian!" shouted Mr and Mrs Austin in unison.

"Brian's been skiving, Brian's been skiving," Ben sang, laughing at the top of his voice. "Every Friday, and he forges Mum's signature onto a fake sick note."

With a growl of rage, Brian launched himself across the table at Ben, and grabbed him by the throat. Ben's chair crashed over backwards, carrying both boys with it, but Brian held his grip on Ben's throat. Ben began to gag and choke, but Brian squeezed even tighter. Mr and Mrs Austin tried to pull him off, but he was too strong for them.

Mrs Austin screamed into Brian's ear, begging him to let go. He did let go, with one hand. He smacked his mother so hard across the face that she was sent sprawling onto the floor. She lay there stunned, but before Mr Austin was able to hold his arm down, Brian had his brother by the throat with both hands again.

To his horror, Mr Austin saw that Ben was going blue in the face. He had to do something fast. Feeling sick, with the side of his clenched fist, he whacked Brian hard across the side of the head.

Brian held on. He turned his head towards his father and his lip curled back. There was a horrible drool all around his mouth. "You'll pay for that," he hissed.

Mr Austin realised that his younger son did not have much time left. Brian had gone mad, and fast action was required to save the younger boy. He kicked Brian as hard as he could in the side of the head. With a growl, this time the older boy was knocked over, but he recovered quickly, and moved back towards the motionless Ben.

Mr Austin dived forward and punched Brian as hard as he could, full in the face. Brian went down into a sitting position against the wall and, at last, was still.

Mrs Austin had regained consciousness. She crawled over to where Ben was lying still on the floor. Mr Austin just stood trembling as he saw her check his pulse, then proceed to administer resuscitation.

Suddenly she stood up. "I think he's going to be all right." Sobbing with relief, she dashed off to the telephone.

As Mr Austin heard her dialling, he went to have a look at Brian, and crouched there next to him. A big bruise had developed on the side of his head where he had been kicked, and he still had a look of pain and hatred etched upon his features. His nose was broken and bloody.

Mr Austin sat next to him, placed his arm round the boy's shoulder, drooped his head and sobbed.

His wife returned to the room. "The ambulance is on its way," she announced.

The boys' father looked in her direction, but couldn't see her because of his tears.

"I've killed him," he whispered. "I killed my own son."

Chapter Two

His wet dream came to its exquisite climax, and as it did so, he squirmed and wriggled around in his bed. His back arched to an almost impossible angle, then he collapsed, bouncing happily up and down, a motion which was assisted by his bedsprings. He groaned and moaned aloud but then gradually began to settle down with a relieved, satisfied grin.

He did not wake up, but before he became quiet again, save for a regular, steady breathing, he muttered the words: "Oh, Kirstie, I love you so much."

John Farrell loved Kirstie Harris more than words could say but, tragically , she would never know.

His divorce had not actually become final and, technically, he had still been living under the same roof as his wife when his relationship with Kirstie had begun, and that had proved to be a mistake. He had told Kirstie a lie which he now regretted because he really did love her, but for her it was too late. She felt cheated and used and, in fact, she no longer cared for him very much. His relationship with her had lasted only five months, and he had now not seen her for three months, but he still thought about her, and dreamed about her, all the time. He was infatuated. Besotted.

As he continued to sleep, his dreams flashed back to the happy moment when he plucked up the courage to ask her out. He was a college lecturer, and she a student, although not in any of his classes. She was thirty-one, but she had an air of grace and confidence which far exceeded her years. He had been sitting at a table in the canteen having a cup of coffee right at the end of the lunch break when he heard her soft voice right next to him.

"May I join you?"

John looked up at her and spluttered through a mouthful of coffee.

"Yes, of course."

He pushed a chair out for her and momentarily stood as she sat down.

"Sorry," she laughed. "There was nowhere else."

On looking around John noticed there were dozens of empty seats all over the place. In fact the canteen was rapidly becoming more empty as people stood up and rushed off to their next lessons.

"Yes, indeed!"

He looked at this young woman and noticed how she appeared to be gazing at him, as if trying to discover what lay behind his eyes. She, he thought, was quite gorgeous. She had a cute, round, plumpish sort of face, with the rosiest cheeks he had ever seen, the reddest lips without a hint of lipstick or any other make-up and, in total contrast, the lightest, bluest eyes. Glancing further down he noticed that the top of her blouse was sufficiently unbuttoned to allow a glimpse of the top of a very generous pair of breasts.

She smiled, and coughed politely, having enjoyed the way he was obviously admiring her, then prodded his leg with her foot under the table.

"Oh, yes, er, sorry."

He grinned awkwardly and met her eye to eye across the table.

"So what is it you teach?" she asked, and with her elbows on the table she rested her chin demurely on her hands.

"Computer studies," he replied, but looking up he noticed he was already late for his next class. "I could tell you all about it, but it will have to be some other time. Maybe we could meet up for a drink."

"Love to," came her reply, with the prettiest smile.

Again he said something in his sleep, and rolled over. He gave his pillow a tender, moist kiss, and said, "Kirstie, my darling," then he settled down again. With a little sigh, his dreams rapidly travelled off once more, taking him this time to the excitement of their first date.

He had fancied Kirstie, and had been fantasising over her for so long, he wanted to make the very best impression possible. He was very slightly on the heavy side of medium build, but with a more than respectable height of six-foot-one, he was confident enough with his general appearance. He had short, dark hair, and, for the last fifteen years, ever since his late teens, he had kept a neat, full beard, but before meeting Kirstie again he had decided to give it a good trim. Finally, he decided to shave the whole thing off, as he had heard her making some unfavourable comments about kissing men with beards, and he definitely wanted to kiss her on their first date.

He arrived at The Highwayman at 8.20 p.m. even though he had not arranged to meet her until 8.30 p.m., so he had time to visit the men's room and check himself in the mirror. When he went to the bar she was already there waiting for him and, for a moment, it did not occur to him that she may have difficulty in recognising him now he'd shaved off his beard, but when he approached her and said, "Kirstie," she turned her head and just looked at him for several seconds. Then, when she spoke she brushed the back of her hand down the side of his face.

"Where's it all gone, then?" she smiled.

"It's a long story."

He led her to a table in the corner where they could talk quietly, and within minutes they were holding hands. Everything seemed so perfect and natural between them, and a couple of hours later when they left together, they joined in a warm embrace - cuddling and kissing each other passionately on the lips. It was when he pushed his tongue into her mouth that she only gently moved away, but then asked him if he would like to come to her house for a cup of coffee. He, of course, had gratefully accepted.

He shook his head crossly as the clock radio began with an appalling mixture of music and bleeper. He was cross because that beautiful dream had turned out to be nothing more than just that - a dream, and to make it ten times worse, the telephone began ringing at precisely the same moment. He answered it while the radio was still on.

"Just wait a minute," he barked. He switched off the clock-radio. "Hello," he said into the receiver in more measured tones.

"John?"

'Shit!' he whispered to himself. It was Lou, his ex-wife.

"What?"

"Sorry, hun," he said sweetly. "What is it, my dearest?"

"I'm just phoning to say that I've received my electricity and gas bills - red ones - and you promised to pay all this for the first twelve months or until I get a job."

"Okay, my sweetness," John sang. "Send them to me."

He hung up the telephone, leaned back on his pillow with one arm across his forehead and puffed out his cheeks while trying to remember why he ever got married. With a hefty, sad sigh, he began to think about his dream and wondered if he would ever forget about Kirstie. She had been like no other girl he had ever been with.

Tears began to well up in his eyes as he lay there continuing to think about all the wonderful times he had spent with Kirstie; not just sexually, but generally, and the time he had spent with her and her children had been wonderful. He had been convinced that she had felt something for him also. She had two young children from a previous marriage, and a baby from a recent relationship, and he himself had a young daughter. They all got on so well together as one big, happy family and it had been her idea for them all to go away together for a short holiday but, strangely, it was very soon after this he detected doubts creeping in and her attitude seemed to change.

One night, though, he took her out to dinner, mainly so he could talk to her quietly, and tell her how he was feeling - that he was falling in love with her. She seemed to gradually change back to the loving, affectionate girl he had first made love to nearly five months earlier. When they arrived back at her house, she relieved her babysitters, and when she led John by the hand up to her bed they made love in the tenderest, most caring sort of way. He wanted to care for her, to protect her, and he would have killed, or been killed, for her, all he wanted in return was to be with her.

But a week later, she did not want anything to do with him. She wrote a brief letter to him telling him that she felt used and cheated. He left messages on her answerphone which she ignored. He kept writing to her, begging her for a chance to explain, but she never replied. He even went to her house, but she did not come to the door, even though he strongly suspected that she was there.

All of a sudden he sat up and shook his head as if to clear his brain. Not for the first time he was cross with himself for continuing this self torture. He would have to get Kirstie out of his head. It was easier said than done because he still loved her so much, but he knew he would have to try.

As he started to get dressed he became aware that it was raining quite heavily. It was the beginning of spring but there had been an unusually large amount of rain lately and he swore at himself as he remembered that there were still a few socks and shirts outside on the washing line. Not having a woman around was a pain in the arse. A reliable woman, he felt, would not have left washing out overnight.

He finished dressing, then went downstairs deep in thought. Years ago you could have safely left your washing out in the rain, happy even that it was getting a clean, fresh rinse, but you couldn't do that with the filthy muck that fell from the skies these days. He quickly pulled on a coat from the peg, deciding that all the clothes from the line would have to be washed again.

As he was outside, unpegging some sopping wet socks, a movement caught his eye from the corner of his garden. It was some sort of small animal. Then, quite clearly, he saw it hopping. It was a frog. Just an ordinary frog.

He went to have a closer look, then he saw another one, and then another. In surprise, he started counting the creatures that he had never seen in his garden before. There were seven frogs sitting in the flower bed in the corner of his garden. He shook his head as water from his rain-soaked hair began running into his eyes. He estimated that his garden was at least a mile from the riverbank, but there had been so much rain that the frogs had obviously got confused. Also, he had heard of frogs which had travelled much further away from any river, but he wouldn't have thought that they would survive too long if the weather suddenly dried up.

Thinking no more of it, he finished collecting his washing, went inside and threw everything back into the washing machine. Next he got his egg-poaching pan out to begin preparing breakfast, filled up the kettle, and turned on the radio. And there, on the radio, was a record playing which had been number one when he was with Kirstie. The lyrics were all about having found the girl of your dreams, and wanting to be with her forever.

He sat on a stool in the kitchen and, with his eyes glistening, listened, and decided he needed time away somewhere. Time to think, to plan. "Time out," as Kirstie would have called it. Holding his face in his hands the music on the radio continued, and with his eyes squeezed tightly shut he could still see Kirstie's beautiful, smiling face.

At that moment, he believed he could never possibly fall in love again.

Many weeks went by, time spent wallowing in the muddy depths of the doldrums, before John's life started to take on a new sense of direction once again. His ex-wife started a new career of her own and had now left him with Sam, their five year-old daughter. He loved his little daughter so much there was nothing he would not do for her, so having gone through a somewhat transitional period in life, he was beginning to feel that he was getting back onto the right track.

In the love-life department, his affair with Kirstie Harris had left him feeling emotionally scarred, and his whole philosophy about women had dramatically changed. He could not believe the putrid sequence of events which had occurred and, although partly his fault, he could scarcely understand or accept how such a wonderful relationship with a loving woman had ended up with this tribulation. Whereas he would have done anything for the woman he loved, he would from now onwards demand that they did more for him. He couldn't help it, but practically every female who appeared to him between the age of seventeen and forty-three he saw as a chance for a possible relationship. Moreover, after the final letter he sent to Kirstie, pleading with her to let him back into her life, he decided that, in future, as far as romance was concerned, he would be out purely for what he could get. A philosophical friend of his had once said that other people often disappointed him, and occasionally he would disappoint other people, but he would never, ever disappoint himself. John decided that, from now on, he would be like that.

That morning he was searching for a present for Sam's sixth birthday, and he decided to go into the town near where he lived. Because of the continual rise in unemployment since the early 1990's, Bedford had become a ghost town. There was only one good employer left and that was Allen's, a medium sized factory which made locks, bolts and hinges. There were also a few shops left. John came across this one place - a pet shop just on the outskirts of the town centre. Bet's Pets. He went in.

There were five other people in the shop. One was an elderly man with a horrible poodle pulling on its leash. It tugged urgently towards the door as John Farrell went through it. The old man seemed to succumb to the irritable dog's wish to leave the shop and followed it through the door practically pushing John out of the way.

"That's all right," John said loudly to the old man, even though there was no apology. He smiled at the thought that dogs and their owners looked strangely similar. Both man and dog were short, fat and elderly, but whereas the dog had a stupid tuft of curls on its head, like an aigrette, the man was as bald as a ping-pong ball.

And then there were only four people in the shop.

Two boys of about fourteen were looking at two white creatures in a cage and, for some reason, laughing.

"No," one of the boys was saying, "it is Siberian hamster."

Both boys broke out into fresh bouts of laughter. John went to see what creatures could cause such fun, then with a smile he understood. Rats, and the comic line originally came from Manuel in *Fawlty Towers*. But these, of course, were white rats and people frequently kept them as pets.

John assumed that the lady at the counter was called Bet. She was neat enough but he guessed her to be about forty-five and, therefore, too old for him. The remaining person, however, a very young woman in her early twenties, was gorgeous. He stood there admiring her fantastic figure in her tight, red, mini skirt. She wore a silky blouse which was open at the top just to reveal the shapes of two, fairly small, but extremely firm and proud little breasts. The sleeves, instead of being short, were long but rolled up to just below the elbows. John, for some reason, always thought that rolled up sleeves on a woman looked amazingly sexy, especially when she placed her hands on her hips. As if the young woman was a mind-reader, she placed one hand on her hip, and slanted her body over to one side as she peered into a huge glass case at some reptilian creature. As she did this, her mini skirt rose slightly revealing more of her beautifully shaped legs which were bare. She looked round for a moment, and John was able to take a brief look at her face and was fascinated at how pretty she was. She had the sort of face that a man would keep on having to take a fresh look at so that he could judge each of her features properly. With a heart-shaped face, high cheekbones, rosebud lips and the largest eyes, she was a classic beauty.

Then, as the girl took an even closer look at the reptile in the glass case, John momentarily was able to view the cheekiness of her bottom but then something totally strange and unexpected happened. Quite quickly the girl lifted the top off the reptile's glass case, reached in and grabbed the creature, which happened to be a four-foot-long orange ratsnake, and hurled it across the counter at the woman. The middle-aged woman threw up her arms in horror and screamed, and backed away clumsily, crashing into shelves behind her knocking over dozens of bags of budgerigar food, then fell over backwards with the snake wrapped around her knees. Budgies, parrots and monkeys all began screeching hysterically. Immediately afterwards, the door opened and another woman in her forties came in with a beaming smile which changed to a startled expression as she saw the commotion in the shop.

"Dear me, Cath," she wailed with her hand on her mouth. "What the..."

"Oh, Bet!" cried the woman, gingerly picking up the harmless snake, then getting up off the floor herself. "That horrible girl just threw it at me."

The young girl and the two boys were all laughing.

"Oh, Sue," said the one who was obviously Bet. "You really are awful sometimes. Don't you ever get tired of your silly practical jokes?"

"Not ever," replied Sue. "And anyway, if Auntie Cath is going to take over the shop she should learn how to handle *all* the creatures."

"I'll get you for that!" Cath said breathlessly, and actually smiling as she put the ratsnake back into its case. "I know what you're scared of - spiders."

"Ah," Sue grimaced. "You just keep those bird-eaters away from me."

They all laughed.

"Er, excuse me," said John. "I wonder if you have any baby rabbits. I want one for my daughter's birthday which is next Sunday."

"Not at the moment I'm afraid," said Bet. "How about a nice hamster?"

John thought for a moment. "I'll tell you what. There's one other place I might try today for a baby rabbit. If they haven't got any I'll be back for a hamster."

"Okay. Bye."

On his way out of the shop, John Farrell passed the glass case where the huge bird-eating spiders were kept for those interested in exotic pets. He lifted the top, picked out one of the wriggling creatures and buzzed it across the shop where it landed with a thwack on Sue's chest. He laughed at the blood curdling scream as he walked through the doorway.

Sue Sherringham threw the creature away from herself and ran towards the shop window in time to see John climbing into a silver BMW. She quickly got a pencil and some paper from the counter and jotted down the registration number.

"What are you doing now?" Bet laughed as she put the spider back into his home.

"If the gentleman likes practical jokes..." Sue began.

"Ho ho, look who's talking!"

"Well, anyway," Sue continued, "if he can't find his rabbit I could always deliver his hamster."

"What about a Siberian hamster?" suggested one of the boys. "Or two?"

The other boy laughed as Sue came over to look at the white creatures which were sitting in their cage and sniffing the air as if sensing that their luck was about to change.

Sue smiled at the rats while the boys goggled down her blouse.

"Cute," she said with an evil grin.

Chapter Three

Ethel Hubbard called to her dogs for the fourth time, and still they ignored her. Every morning before breakfast, she took her three Alsatians for a run by the river so they could all work up an appetite. She was in her sixties now and, although she was of a very sight build, she had always owned alsations and found them to be very loyal, gentle and protective. They were also, usually, obedient.

As she called them again, she began to walk towards them, and noticed, with some amusement, that they appeared to have found some small animal to play with.

'Poor thing,' she laughed softly to herself. It was a frog. She saw it hopping as each dog went to prod at it, but for some reason they kept on backing away from it, snarling.

Then it leaped into the air, and the dogs chased around in circles. From a distance, Ethel had been unable to see where it had gone. "Well I never," she panted as she trotted towards her dogs. Again she called them, and this time they came to her but, for some reason, she noticed they all seemed to be sneezing, and sniffing, and shaking their heads.

An hour later, she was at home, cooking breakfast for herself, and preparing a good snack for the dogs. They were in the garden but they seemed unusually quiet considering that they knew that they were about to be fed.

She went out from the kitchen holding two bowls of food.

The first dog attacked before she had time to place the food on the ground. It jumped onto her back and bit deeply into her neck. It tasted blood, and began mauling her savagely. As she screamed in agony, the second dog went for her legs and started to tear flesh and muscle before she fell to the ground. The first dog had bitten into her jugular vein. There was a fountain of blood, but before she bled to death, the third dog actually went to protect her from the other two. It clawed and bit into the first dog's back, but then the other two dogs, together, turned on the third one. It put up a good fight on its own, but in the end, two against one was too much for it. It tried to run away, carrying with it many serious wounds, but the other two kept up the ferocious attack until it was so weak that it collapsed, bleeding terribly.

Then the other two dogs set upon each other and kept fighting until they were both so badly hurt and exhausted, that they, too, collapsed. Ethel Hubbard was already dead, and soon, all her dogs were dead as well.

Kirstie Harris normally enjoyed the luxury of her latest boyfriend, David Conner, collecting her from her own house in his comfortable Jag. But this evening, she telephoned him telling him that she would meet him in the town. Having made the necessary arrangements with her babysitters, she then caught the bus arriving in town a little before eight o'clock - more than half an hour before she had arranged to meet David Conner.

She decided to go for a walk by the river. On this spring evening it was still fairly light, but the red lamps by the pathway were already illuminated, making attractive reflections in the rippling water. Also, following some very heavy rain they'd had earlier that day, the weather seemed as though it was going to dry up now. She walked slowly and, with her hands resting in the pockets of her white jacket, she was deep in thought.

She remembered a very romantic evening she'd had with her last boyfriend. They went for a meal in town, then before going home they had walked for a while along this very path. But that relationship had not lasted. In fact, it had been some considerable time since she had been in a relationship which had lasted more than six months. It was not that the boys got tired of her. Far from it. At thirty-one she was a very attractive young woman, and her last boyfriend, John, had told her that he loved her and wanted to be with her forever. With a hefty sigh she realised that she could no longer accept all this 'love' and 'forever' business, especially when she found that the man had been lying to her about being divorced. After that initial shock, even though his pending divorce had eventually gone through, for her it was over. As soon as a boyfriend started to talk in this way, she found herself losing trust and faith. It was weird, but at the same time, ultimately, what she needed from a relationship was to be loved. She knew she had a problem but she could not work out the answer.

Seven years earlier, she had got married. The fact that she had become pregnant prior to this did not matter. At least it was the father of the child who still cared for her, and loved her, and it was he who had wanted to marry her. And so they were married, and just six months later she gave birth to a lovely little boy, and they named the little boy Kimble. Neither she, nor her new husband, or any of their parents, could afford to give them a terrific starter home, but her parents put nearly all of their savings together and, with all of her savings, they were able to put down a modest deposit on a two bedroom, co-ownership flat. Her new husband, Ian, seemed slightly embarrassed at the fact that neither he, nor his parents, had been able to contribute anything at all, but she assured him that it was okay, just so long as they were happy and, the main thing was, they were together. And, she believed, they were happy, and when two years later she had another beautiful child, a little girl this time, she could not imagine greater happiness. And they named the little girl Melanie after her mother.

The first warning signals were Ian frequently arriving home late from work, but she hardly noticed. She had been so busy during the day with general household chores, coupled with looking after two young children, that she was too tired to notice. They rarely talked about what they had each done during the day, so in retrospect, she thought, one of their problems may have simply been lack of communication. Maybe an argument here and there would have been better than not to have communicated at all, but Ian's father had been a cantankerous old sod, and she was only glad that Ian did not appear to have taken after him. Anyway, his excuse of having to work late meant that she would merely go to bed early, and leave him to do his own cooking.

This she found acceptable at first, and even had time to laugh at the amount of washing up there was to be done the following morning. He never did the washing up, and although she considered that he might have worked quite hard at the office, at home, she believed, he was a lazy layabout and never helped around the house, but she loved him so much and was still so happy and willing to put up with his many idiosyncrasies, that she did not think it mattered much.

Then, the mess in the kitchen stopped. She asked him about this, and he said that he had realised at long last that it was unfair to saddle her with all his washing up, so he had done it himself. Then she became suspicious, and waited up one night. He rolled in at about midnight, and came straight up to bed without eating anything. The following morning she asked him what time he got in, and he told her about 10.30 p.m. She asked him about his dinner, because she noticed that nothing seemed to have been used, and he told her that he had got a bite to eat out somewhere.

His interest in making love to her was also on the decrease, but by the time she had really begun to worry, her marriage was over. He came home from work one day (on time for a change) but only to tell her that it was over. He'd had enough, and he was off. It was so sudden, she was shocked. And, that evening, he left.

Within a week she realised that he had not got his own place, but he was actually living with another woman. Then the wife of one of his friends at work let on that he had been seeing this woman for ages - at least a year. One day, she was out shopping and bumped into Ian's best man whom she had not seen for a couple of years. At the mention of this woman, he informed her that Ian had known her long before they even got married. One month later, Ian told her himself, that as soon as their divorce was through, he was going to marry this woman.

The last straw came when Kirstie actually met her. The woman had the nerve to follow Ian into the house while he was collecting the last of his personal belongings. She was twittering on, taking about their new home, and it transpired that Ian's parents were helping them buy the house, by giving them a huge sum of money. Kirstie felt hurt and angry. In the kitchen there was a full kettle of water which had just boiled, and she was so close to rushing at this horrible little cheat, and tipping the entire contents of the kettle over her head. Of course, she resisted the temptation, but the thought of it, that her mum and dad had given up nearly all their savings to give Kirstie and Ian this little flat, and all that time his parents were sitting there on thousands of pounds which they wouldn't lend to them, but were quite happy to now that he was with this little tramp. It was only then that she woke up to how captious his parents had always been towards her, and began to recall instances which indicated that they never really liked her. They did not feel that she was good enough for their little Ian.

Coupled with how influenced Ian was by them, and how domineering they were over him, Kirstie had dolorously concluded that the break-up of her marriage was, after all, largely the fault of Ian's parents.

She was on her own for three years until her children were aged six and four. Then she met David. It was, she believed, love at first sight. He was so charming, and generous, he got on with her children really well, and, when at last she let herself go one night, partly because she had not had sex, or experienced all the emotions that go with it for so long, he proved to be a very fulfilling, and satisfying lover.

When, two months later, he proposed marriage to her, it was, coincidentally, the day after she found she was pregnant. She asked him what he thought of having more children, and he seemed moderately interested in the idea. "Sometime in the future, sure," was his actual answer, but she was so overjoyed, that she hit him with the wonderful news. She was sure he seemed okay about it. They continued to talk lovingly about their future together with the three children, and about where they would get married. Then he made some excuse about having to get away early that evening because he had an early start for the following morning, so they kissed and said goodbye.

And then, David Conner disappeared. She could not find him at home, his telephone was disconnected, and whenever she went to his flat, she could not get an answer. She did for a while consider having an abortion, but she was a strong believer in the unborn child having the right to live. Right up until the child was due to be born, her friends and family tried to find David, but to no avail. The whole affair had left her feeling sickened. For a time he had been loving and generous, but she had been merely his courtesan to enjoy, to use, but with no responsibility.

So now she had three children, and no trust in any man. About eight months ago, she had met John at college. He had seemed an honest, reliable sort of guy who was getting divorced, and had a child of his own. He also got on with her children extremely well, but when he started going on about falling in love with her, and wanting to be with her forever, she just thought: 'Oh no, here we go again!' Besides, there had been something decidedly fishy about his divorce. His wife was divorcing him, evidently for unreasonable behaviour, but they were still living together. When she was clear to apply for the decree absolute, she refused to apply, then when the date finally arrived whereby he could apply, inexplicably, there still appeared to be a delay. Clearly, there was more than a hint of hesitancy and uncertainty.

All of a sudden, David turned up again. He was sorry, he had been confused, he wanted to see his child - now a year old, and he wanted them to be one big happy family. Despite promising John that they would continue to see each other as soon as his divorce was final, she decided that, for her, after all, this was the way to go and she felt strongly that he had broken a promise to her concerning the absolute certainty of his divorce. Another undertaking that she and John had made, which had been her idea, was that because she had been hurt so frequently in the past she demanded that if, at anytime, he wanted to change the arrangement between them, or if he simply wanted to end it, he should have the decency to tell her straight without messing her around or necessitating a lot of guesswork. She, of course, had promised to adhere to the same rule. Unfortunately, when Conner arrived back on the scene, she was so confused and scared that she just dropped John without really telling him anything. She had been afraid to reply to his calls, so she just wished that he would forget all about her.

Now though, she was uncertain again. She could not help thinking about the way Conner had deserted her and she began to wonder if she would not be a lot better off by just staying on her own. Men, after all, she concluded, were all totally untrustworthy rats.

She began to walk back along the path, by the river, in the direction she had come from. She arrived at the New Town Hotel just as Conner was getting out of his car.

"Hello," he called to her. "You all right?"

"No, sorry," she replied, going up to him. "We've got to talk."

At the bar of the hotel, Kirstie started the talking, and as she did, she was aware at how fast Conner was drinking, possibly sensing that the volatile Kirstie was about to make one of her notorious, about turn decisions.

"We've been going back and forth for so long," she found herself saying, "and things are just different now."

'He seems to be taking this all so well', she thought. A little too well, if not quietly, but suddenly he seemed keen on changing the subject, then actually taking her home before he became too drunk to drive.

"Maybe we should get a taxi," she suggested.

"I'm off," he said, abruptly getting up. "You coming?"

He drove her home, then she made the mistake of inviting him in for a strong, black cup of coffee. At the sight of Conner, the babysitters reluctantly left, but were assured by Kirstie that everything was fine. For quite a while afterwards, Conner just sat in silence, drinking his coffee.

Then he said: "So all the promises you made were all lies."

"What promises?" Kirstie stood up, and began to pace slowly up and down the length of the lounge. "And what about the promises you made? Then you disappear, leave me on my own to have the baby, then you reappear. Then you spin a yarn that Hans Christian Andersen would have rejected as a fairy story!"

"So why did you have me back?"

Conner was getting angry, and he threw his half full coffee cup down so that coffee splashed over the carpet.

"I felt I had to," Kirstie blurted out. "I thought I owed something to the children, to give them a responsible father. But look at you. You're not responsible. You're like a little kid yourself, throwing things when you don't get your own way."

"I'm still the father to one of them."

"The best thing I could do for the children now is to stay on my own," she continued, "and do everything for them on my own. We don't need you, or anyone else."

"Until you need another good shafting."

She strode toward him, pointing a finger at him.

"There's only one man who ever made me feel properly loved, but he's..."

"But he's what?" Conner laughed. "Gone off with someone else, has he? Just like Ian did. Don't bloody blame him."

"He really did love me."

She was crying now, and she just stood there, shaking, with her hands held up to her face.

"No one could love you," Conner snarled scornfully. "You're such a selfish little bitch."

Almost blind with her own tears, and motivated by sheer anger, she suddenly launched herself at Conner with her fingernails held out like claws, like a lioness attacking its prey.

Almost blind with her own tears, and motivated by sheer anger, she suddenly launched herself at Conner with her fingernails held out like claws, like a lioness attacking its prey.

He received a quadruple groove down one side of his face which oozed blood, but he deflected her bodyweight with his elbow which rescued his eyes and sent her off balance.

"You whore!" he roared, then he slapped her hard across the face with one hand, and punched her in the mouth with the other. She fell over backwards and lay still.

At first he just stood over her, nervously licking his lips, as if worried that he might have killed her. But he breathed a sigh of relief when she moved slightly, moaned, and moved her arm across her face.

"You bastard!" she whispered. "Thank God I didn't go through with this. What a mistake! I pity the poor woman who ever marries you!"

"You stupid bitch!" Conner laughed. "I am married."

Kirstie just looked at him, angry and disbelieving. Then she slowly began to get to her feet.

"Just get out," she said quietly, "before I call the police. Get out and never come back."

Just then there was a knock at the door, and a woman's voice shouting.

"Kirst, are you okay?"

It was Nikki from next door.

Without a word, David Conner dashed to the kitchen, and made his way out through the back door.

It was beginning to rain heavily again now, and in the lamplight from the street he could just make out some movement in the back garden. He paused only very briefly to study the strange sight. A whole lot of frogs appeared to be grouped together in the back garden, and as he ran through the gate and into the street, he saw more of them on the pathway. He climbed into his car, but before driving off, still with his head spinning from too much alcohol, he was sure he heard some of the frogs squeaking more like mice, amongst the others that croaked normally.

He sure hoped he wasn't pulled in by the law, he thought, chuckling to himself. He must be pissed.

Chapter Four

Desmond Prickett looked gloomily into his pint of beer as if there was something wrong with it.

"Sacked," he breathed. "Cast aside like a used dishcloth they needed not."

Alan Brynn, his best mate, regarded him with a sympathetic smile from the opposite side of the little table. At thirty he was six years younger than Des, had a degree in Biology and various other skills and qualifications so he was quite confident of finding more work since the redundancies. Moreover, he did not have a mortgage and other debts that his friend had.

"Don't worry, something will turn up, it always does?"

"Yeah? Well, sure. Like what?"

"Like I've got an idea." Alan took a sip from his pint of bitter, then banged the glass down on the table, making Des jump and sit up. "It's one hell of an idea. I've been working on it since long before we even heard that the Pest Control Department was cutting back, and if you help me this idea will give us plenty of well paid work."

Des took a long drink from his pint jug, placed the glass quietly down between them, wiped his mouth with the back of his hand and then looked at his friend.

"Okay , tell me."

"People would call Pest Control if they had problems with wasps, or slugs, or..."

"Bats in the belfry - have another drink."

"Could be bats, or ants, or..." He looked more closely at Des as though the answer was etched there on his nose, "rats!"

"Rats?"

Des shook his head then drained his glass.

Alan did the same then held his glass up.

"Did you say another?"

"Here I'll get 'em in."

Des grunted and burped, and then accidentally farted as he stood up. It was getting late, about 10.45 p.m., and the two mates had been sitting drinking since eight. They'd already had seven pints each and both were beginning to look very red in the face. While Des was up at the bar he looked back towards his friend and smiled when he saw that Alan's attention was currently taken by a really cute, very slightly plump brunette with a short skirt and ample breasts. Unfortunately, she looked like she was already spoken for and her boyfriend did not look like the type you generally crossed swords with. He looked like the kind who could lift a ton but couldn't spell it, but then again a lot of girls liked blokes like that. They liked the primitive types, he concluded. The ones who tended to make "Uhg, uhg," noises at each other instead of embarking upon a lot of intellectual conversation. As Des paid for the drinks he began to think about Alan's curious remarks about the Pest Control Department. Of the two mates, Alan was definitely the more audacious, whereas Des preferred to think things through almost tentatively. He also thought it amusing that Alan, like so many other people that he knew, ranted on after they'd had a few drinks. He had a girlfriend like that once. He'd had a terrible argument with her after she'd been on the gin. To this day he could not remember what the argument had been about, so maybe he was the one who had been groggy on that occasion and it had been all his fault, but the following day she was saying how sorry she was for going on, and how the drink had muddled her thinking. He believed, though, that drink was like a truth drug, and people only started describing their real feelings when they were slightly pissed. For that reason they had no right to say how sorry they were for the night before, that is, of course, if they could remember, simply because they were embarrassed about disclosing their innermost secrets.

He returned to his seat, dropped a bag of peanuts on the table, put down the drinks and sat down.

"Okay, now tell me this story."

Alan took a gulp of beer, and then began to open the bag of peanuts.

"I've been working on an incredible project," he told Des. "Rats, I've been breeding them."

"Oh, I get you. Sell 'em as pets. Yeah, good one."

"These won't be pets," Alan said quietly. "People will want to get rid of them. People will get them, and be so mad to get rid of them, that when we conveniently show up they'll pay us to kill them."

"And what's to stop Ratkill from coming along to solve the problem first?" Des asked with an incredulous expression on his face.

"Oh, they'll try alright," Alan laughed, noisily relieving himself of some eructation. "But these are not just ordinary rats. I've done something so that only I know how to deal with them. They're mutations. Well, actually, hybrids."

Des sat back in amazement.

"You must be drunk, or maybe I am, for listening to all of this maunder."

Alan grabbed a handful of peanuts, voraciously pushed a huge quantity of them into his mouth and began munching with a happy grin upon his features.

"What if they breed so fast you can't handle them?" Des continued.

"Ah ha," Alan chortled. "I've thought of that one. All the specimens that I release into people's cellars and barns will be specially treated so that they cannot reproduce."

"And what's so different about these creatures that they won't be affected by rat poison?"

"By pure chance, I found a creature which is about the same size as a small rat, it's fast, it's agile, it leaps - boy it can practically fly..."

"Fly?" Des sat in wonder. "You're kidding, but what..."

"Yes," Alan asserted holding up his hand, "it's impervious to rat poisons, but I somehow accidentally produced a cross between this creature and a common, black rat. The offspring are really incredible, ugly little bastards. I think the cage of a pregnant rat was somehow contaminated with... Well, like I said, we could release these things into people's gardens, then for an exorbitant price we would come along and exterminate the little devils. We could call ourselves The Ratbusters, or something like that."

"Okay, okay." Des had had enough of the suspense. "So what *is* this creature?"

Alan paused for a moment, then he spoke slowly and quietly. "You know my old uncle who owns the greengrocers in Bedford? Well, a couple of months ago, he called me urgently, telling me he'd got something I'd be interested in. I went over and it turned out that when he opened this crate of bananas from Jamaica, out leaped this frog."

"A frog? That's your creature?"

"Not just any old frog," Alan said indignantly. "This is a West Indian tree frog, a horrible little green and yellow thing."

"But they're poisonous aren't they?"

"Yes, but that's okay."

"You crazy fucker," Des stormed in fulmination. "That's not okay!"

Alan was indignant again.

"Des, do you honestly think I'd release poisonous animals all over the countryside? Firstly, I have so far not seen any evidence that the babies are going to be at all venomous, although they do look a bit strange, and secondly I've still got these creatures locked up securely and I'm still doing tests on them."

"So finish your tests," Des said, "and then destroy the lot of them."

What Alan did not tell Des, was that when his uncle had called him, there had been two tree frogs, but unfortunately one escaped before Alan arrived. He did not think that it mattered now, though. There had been no reports of anything in the two months since, so he assumed that the thing had died in an environment which would not suit it.

Alan finished his drink.

"Look, wouldn't you like to come over to my house and see them?"

"Your house? You've got them in..."

"Well, actually, they're in my garden shed."

Des finished his drink, then consumed the last few peanuts.

"I suppose I should take a look."

"Great. Let's go."

When they arrived back at Alan's home, Alan picked up a torch from the garage which was in a block to the side of the house. The two men went down the footpath which led to Alan's garden. It was almost pitch dark and Alan switched on the torch, and swung the beam of light to the end of his garden.

"There's my shed," he said in a soft voice. "There's my..."

He stopped so suddenly that Des walked right into the back of him.
"What's up?" Des asked.

Alan didn't answer, he just broke into a run, going down the garden towards his shed. Des ran as well, following the light in front of him.

"What's wrong?" he said breathlessly when they reached the shed.

"Shit, look!" Alan put the light of the torch onto the shed door. There was a large, jagged hole in the middle of it.

Des stood silently while Alan fished in his pocket for the keys to the shed. At last the door was open, they stepped inside and Alan switched on an overhead lamp.

The two men stared at the half dozen empty cages with their mesh doors chewed open.

"Oh, shit!" Alan hissed as his worst fears were realised. He grasped hold of the edge of a shelf to steady himself and gazed around the shed in dismay. "They're gone!"

Chapter Five

It had been beautiful around the Bedford countryside earlier during that spring, but that brilliant sunshine seemed to be gone forever. Rain had been falling continuously for two full days now, and the weather men had already stated that there were no signs yet of any improvement.

There were aspects of a good rain storm which Sue Sherringham did enjoy. For instance, lying in her warm, cosy bed late at night and listening to the heavy rain as thunder reverberated around her house. The flashes of lightening would light up her bedroom, and she actually found this to be quite therapeutic. There were aspects of bad weather, though, that she did not like. For example, driving in it, and as the heavy rain continued to fall, making an unpleasantly harsh sound on the soft top of her sports car, she listened intently to the weather forecast on the car's radio.

"Continued heavy rain and thunder storms could make driving treacherous," (she already knew that) "and some roads in Bedfordshire, Hertfordshire and Cambridgeshire are already blocked."

She switched on the heater, directing warm air onto the windscreen to avoid mist, and as she turned her windscreen wipers on to full speed, she began to have regrets about this outing. She had wanted to test the old adage: "he (or she) who laughs last," but now she did not feel quite as keen. Not often had one of her schemes backfired on her, and this one hadn't as yet, but there was a grave danger of it doing so if she was not going to be able to see where she was going. Her pertinacity, along with her wish to level the score, could yet get her into deep water in more ways than one.

The water from a huge puddle hit the underside of her car with a resounding slap, and she decreased her speed to fifteen miles per hour. She peered desperately through her windscreen hoping for a road sign or some other clue as to where she was, but to no avail.

Yes, she was definitely regretting this journey, and the whole scheme which could easily have waited for another day.

Sue Sherringham had not forgotten Mr Farrell's little joke of throwing that horrible spider at her. She had always been a bit of a jester herself and she laughed aloud as she remembered how daft old Auntie Cath had reeled and fallen over backwards with a ratsnake wrapped around her. But then John Farrell had stolen the show with his spider trick before leaving the pet shop.

Actually, he had seemed like a good sort of bloke, one who had a great sense of humour and could give her a good laugh. She was even excited at the prospect of seeing him again, but had decided that before a relationship could develop, she would have to settle the score. So far it was one-nil to him. She was glad that she'd had the presence of mind to take his car registration number, for that evening she arranged a night out with the girls after making sure that her best friend Tracey Clarke was off duty.

Sue and Tracey had both applied to go into the police together some years ago and had both been successful in their entrance tests. Together they went on a two-day assessment where they took tests (more difficult than the first) and were given tasks, some to be completed on their own, while others were to be done as teamwork with the fifteen men and women who were also on the assessment. In addition, they were given gruelling examinations in physical fitness which she had prepared for by running six miles a day and doing a hundred sit-ups and press-ups each day for the previous six months. Finally, she had an interview with the Chief Constable of the force.

It was at that last hurdle that she had fallen. The Chief first congratulated her on doing so well, especially in physical fitness where she had been assessed as the best woman, even achieving a better time in her running than some of the men. But without delving too deeply into the whys and wherefores, he considered her not to be perfectly cut out for the job mentally. He did, however, hasten to add that he didn't mean that she was stupid, quite intelligent in fact, but still not totally suited to the job of police officer.

Sue, of course, was very disappointed. She had grown tired of the mundane, quotidian kind of existence that all her previous jobs had tended to offer, and had set her heart on becoming a WPC. Tracey, though, continued to be extremely supportive towards her, and, having successfully got through her own assessment, she promised to do all she could to help her friend. Her training started just three weeks later - a ten week stint at Shotley Gate, and in her first letter to Sue from training college she reiterated her desire to do anything to help her friend. What she had meant by *anything* was any way of assisting her if she wished to reapply to the force, or any other police force, in the future. But when Sue had asked her to look up a car registration number on the PNC (Police National Computer), she hesitated. In the end, though, she obliged; after all there was no great sin involved here, and there were other way of tracing cars, although the police computer was probably the quickest method.

So, Sue Sherringham had found Farrell's address, and soon she would see him again, or so she hoped. Spray from another great pool of water across the road shot up in the air, and the impact of water under the car threatened to stop her right in the middle of it. It was also starting to get quite late and very dark. She was starting to get worried, then two little squeaking sounds from the floor in front of the passenger seat made her remember the purpose of her journey. She stopped the car on the brow of a hill where the puddles weren't too bad, then leaned across the seat next to her. There, in a small cage, were two bristly, white creatures, sniffing the air. They were the two rats from the pet shop. She hoped to find a way of leaving them in a safe place at, or preferably in, John Farrell's house, with a note saying: "Two rats, as ordered by Mr J. Farrell," even though she knew he distinctly said one rabbit and not two rats, "One male together with one female for the purpose of breeding, as requested, specially ordered. Cost for very rare breed of Siberian rats: one thousand pounds."

She smiled to herself, sat upright again, switched on her headlights for it was now getting extremely gloomy, then began driving down the hill. To her surprise, and great relief, she saw a sign pointing to the left which said: Odell 1 mile. That's what she wanted. She was as good as there. She took the left turn and very soon she was outside a lovely old detached cottage. Again she felt regret about not having left this trick for another day. It was still bucketing down and she only had a light plastic cover for the bristly pets. She decided that she would have to take a chance and go up the driveway. She did this as slowly and quietly as she could, but as she drew nearer to the cottage, it seemed that all the lights were out anyway. She switched the car's motor off, reached for her coat behind her, then got out of the car.

Before she took the white rats with her she would check the cottage out. Pulling on her coat and buttoning it up to her neck, she went round the side of the cottage. There, in the failing light, she could just make out the shape of a conservatory or some other type of extension that had been built long after the main building had been erected. She reached the door and tried the handle. To her astonishment, the door was open. She wanted to get this over and done with now, so, with a grin on her face, she went back to the car, and from the passenger's side, took out the rats' cage. At first they squeaked in fright when they felt drops of rain on them, but then Sue quickly pulled the plastic cover over the cage and set off back towards the house. She went through the unlocked door, into the extension, saw a counter or some other type of worktop in the corner and used this to put down the rat's cage with the note stuck on the front of it. She then pulled off the cover before hastily making her way back towards the door. Unfortunately, despite tiptoeing quite surreptitiously in the gloom she kicked over an ironing board which was leaning up against the wall. She jumped as it went down with an almighty crash.

"Shit!" she hissed to herself, still not being absolutely sure if anyone was in or not.

What happened next, she would have great difficulty in piecing together correctly later, for everything happened so fast. She decided to get away quickly. She hurried out, slamming the door noisily behind her, ran back to her car and was opening the car door, when something from the darkness seemed to fly at her and hit her in the side of the face. She put her hand up to her ear and felt a searing pain there as if something was biting her. What she touched made her feel frightened and sick. It was warm and clammy, but bristly as well. She clenched the horrible little body tightly in her fist trying to remove it from her, but it held on, and she could now feel blood tricking down her neck. She screamed and tried to squeeze it even more tightly, deliberately trying to dig her long fingernails into it. Then a second pain tore through the back of her hand.

Just then, she heard someone shout, and a brilliant light dazzled her from the direction of the cottage. A split second before the creatures squealed in fright and jumped away from her to make their retreat, she saw them.

"Rats!" she whispered to herself before the fierce, throbbing pain made her pass out, and before she came round again she had a dream about thousands of small, black creatures swarming over her. They seemed even more horrible because they were clammy and wet.

She thought that must have been because of the rain.

Late that morning, while Sam was at school, John Farrell found himself at home pacing up and down like a caged lion. He was getting really worried and anxious about things all the time. He began to wonder if he was going slightly mad, but try as he might he could not shift Kirstie Harris from his brain. He remembered so vividly the pair of them embraced tenderly in each other's arms. She liked to massage him with plenty of baby oil before they had sex on the floor in her lounge. He recalled the blissful experience of being led by the hand upstairs to her bedroom and being cuddled so warmly by her, then being settled down and lovingly tucked in like a baby, until she got in next to him. The feeling of her wonderful, naked body pressed against him gave him a rock-hard erection. All these memories persisted in flooding back. She had joked around while making love, tickling him and attempting to smother him with her large breasts, making him laugh and come at the same time. She knew how to make love the way it was intended - it was blissful and joyful. It was bloody good fun. Passionately making love again, then talking cosily before peacefully falling asleep in each other's arms, waking up next to her and being led by the hand once again and being bathed by her were all the happiest love-making memories he had ever been given.

But these same memories were now driving him to distraction because they were over. It was all his fault, and he kicked himself for being such a fool. He loved this woman and he had lost her because he had told her one simple lie. Not even that - he had misled her with one carefully told story, and now she would not trust him again. Her husband had previously left her for another woman, another guy had got her pregnant, then buggered off, and now John Farrell was no better than either of them. He could not accept this, or bear the pain any longer.

He would go and see her. It was a twenty-five mile journey to her house, so he could do the journey there and back with, hopefully, at least some talking in between, before collecting Sam from school.

As he sped off in his car, he began to feel better. Even the sight and the sound of the heavy rain could not dampen his newly acquired high spirits. He had made the decision to see her now, and he was on his way so in a little more than half an hour he would be there. Who knows, having convinced her that it was all over now between himself and his wife, he might talk her round to coming back to him. He smiled happily to himself. 'Yeah, why not?' he thought. On the final leg of his journey, however, while driving up her road, he started to get the jitters, and sensed that maybe he was in for one last, big hurt, but he had arrived now and, he knew, if she was in, she might well have already seen him. He parked right outside her house, then strode up her garden path, getting quite wet in the rain, and knocked on the door.

For quite a while there was no answer, but he knocked again, then after three minutes a movement from a curtain caught his attention. He waved and smiled, even though he could not yet see Kirstie's face. After another full minute, he believed that she was simply not going to answer the door, but then, at last, the door slowly opened.

"Oh, John," came a croaky whisper.

"Hi, Kirstie," John started in the lightest voice he could manage despite being soaked to the skin. "I was just passing so I thought I would..."

He broke off when he saw the bruises round one side of her face. He looked more closely and, even in the shadow cast by the doorway, could detect a black bruise round one eye and a swollen lip.

"Jesus!" John gasped in a hoarse voice. "Who did that?"

"Why did you have to come here?"

Firmly but gently John pushed his way in and closed the door. "Who did that?"

"It doesn't matter," Kirstie told him. "Now please go away."

"Not until you tell me who..."

Quietly, someone else appeared in the hallway. John instantly recognised her as Nikki, Kirstie's next door neighbour, a pretty young woman, in her early twenties, and with long, silky brown hair.

"Hello, John," she said softly. "Nice to see you again."

"Likewise," John nodded. "Now will someone tell me what's going on?"

"Why?" Kirstie blurted out. "What's it got to do with you?"

"Kirst, I..."

"Don't say it!" Kirstie opened the door. "Just get out and never come back."

He stepped back out into the pouring rain, and winced at the sound of the slamming door. He paused momentarily, let out a hefty sigh, but with a heavy heart he realised he had very little choice left. He went back down the garden path, and was just getting back into his car when he heard a voice calling behind him. He looked round and saw Nikki running down the path towards him.

"Can you give us a lift?" she asked.

"Sure," he replied glumly. "But you only live next door."

They both got into the car, then she said: "You drive, I'll give directions. We're off to see Kirstie's boyfriend."

"The one who...?"

"Yes. His name's David Conner. He got pissed, apparently. She had very gently tried to give him the elbow after a long relationship."

John's eyes narrowed.

"A long relationship, you say?"

"Oh, yeah," Nikki sighed. "She did meet him before you. He's Nathan's father, but he recently showed up again. She was considering starting with him afresh, but then changed her mind. I think she was trying to explain this to him when he started smacking her around."

"Right." John started to drive. "She told you all this?"

"We heard her screaming. My husband and I went round but this arsehole went running out through the back door."

Nikki was a very good friend of Kirstie's, and she also knew how much John liked her. She even suspected that he was in love with her. She could see how worked up he was about her anyway, and thought that this was the best way of making sure that this other lad, Conner, received his just deserts.

They arrived at Conner's house, stepped out into the pouring rain, and then John stepped to one side as Nikki knocked on the door. After a while a woman answered.

"Oh, good morning," Nikki said sweetly. "Is your husband at home?"

John shook his head sadly. The guy was married.

"Who might you be?" the woman said roughly.

"He asked me to call with a quote," Nikki said cleverly.

Puzzled, the woman went away.

Then, on the doorstep, stood quite a handsome young man, possibly in his late twenties.

"Yes?" he smiled, looking at Nikki who, despite being dripping wet, still looked quite pretty.

"Mr David Conner?" she asked with her sweetest smile.

"Yeah?" he drawled. Obviously not recognising her, he leered at her with a countenance of unbridled lust. "And what can I do for you, my darling?"

But then her pretty smile turned into a snarl.

"You bastard!" she hissed, then backed away.

"You what?" the man stepped out towards her, but then doubled up in agony as the toecap of John's size twelve boot met suddenly with his testicles.

Choking with the dreadful agony, he looked up in time to see a huge fist coming crashing down. He coughed on blood and gagged as his front teeth were broken. His wife reappeared on the scene to witness the second blow which broke her husband's jaw.

"Stop it!" she screamed.

Nikki watched, almost nonchalantly, as John grabbed the man's arm, twisted and lifted it, which raised the man to his feet and broke his arm at the same time. Following the sickening crack, there was hardly a yelp from Conner who was already losing consciousness. He was then pinned up against his own front door before a third punch broke his nose.

Then John just held him by the lapels of his shirt and twisted so that the man could only just breathe. John's face was very close to his when he spoke.

"If you ever go near Kirstie again," he hissed, "I'll come looking for you, and I'll be having very serious words with you."

He then let go and Conner fell to his knees, but still trembling in a blind rage, Farrell continued to shake his fist at the injured man.

"First I'll tear your arms out at the sockets, then I'll rip your legs off, and then I'll knock your fucking head off. Then I'll get really fucking nasty."

John Farrell had never been at all pugnacious, and he soon began to tremble with the realisation of what he had done. He instinctively wanted to protect the woman he loved, and had gone to punish the one who had hurt her. He drove Nikki back to Kirstie's house, but did not go in with her. All he knew was that he loved Kirstie Harris more than ever, but had to accept that she would never love him. He felt no acerbity towards her, but he did consider that life could be a right bitch. He just hoped that one day, maybe, he would learn the reasons why.

Before she got out of the car, Nikki leant across and kissed him lightly on the cheek.

"Goodbye, John," she said quietly, "and thanks."

For all these reasons he had finally decided to have a quiet night in. His daughter, Sam, was in bed, and now he sat relaxing in front of the television with the sound turned low and all the lights out so that, if he felt like it, he could just nod off. It was still four days to go until the party for his daughter's sixth birthday, but he had been very busy and there was still much to do. About twenty children were invited, and his brother and his wife were coming over to help with the inevitable chaos. Also, he had still been unable to find a pet shop who could, at the moment, sell him a baby rabbit for that extra special surprise at Sam's party. Other options did, however, include going back to Bet's Pets and getting a hamster instead. He may even get the opportunity once more of seeing that fabulous looking Sue. Maybe she would help him to keep his mind off Kirstie. He smiled at the recollection of the little joke he'd played on her, then dismissed any idea he might have had about asking her out.

"Sorry about my little joke putting that giant spider down inside your bra, but anyway I wondered if you liked the idea of having lunch with me..." No, there had to be more chance of getting a date with Catherine Zeta Jones or Linda Lusardi. He sat there pondering over pictures of other beautiful girls in his mind's eye, when he heard the most awful crash from the kitchen. It sounded like he had burglars because he was sure he heard the sound of scampering feet and the door to the extension slamming afterwards. He dashed to the back door, grabbed his torch which he kept attached to the wall next to the door, then raced out into the pouring rain. The torch was a long, heavy one which could be used as a truncheon if necessary. Then he thought he heard a scream. A woman's scream. Christ, what was happening? He knew that there was such a thing as a female burglar, but... He reached the top of the driveway and shone his torch towards the gate, half expecting to see a woman like Michele Pfeiffer dressed in a catsuit somersaulting around the corner. What he saw was a girl who looked familiar, dressed in a mid-length raincoat, standing next to a sportscar which was parked on his drive. But it was not the unfamiliar sportscar parked on his property that shocked him. It was the girl, because she seemed to be struggling with something horrible attached to her face.

"Hey, what's happening?" he yelled, pointing the beam of light directly onto the stricken girl.

Then, two creatures hopped onto the ground. He lunged towards the girl as she wobbled on her feet, and caught her as she fell. In the pouring rain he knelt down with her and saw that she was bleeding. He could still see the strange-looking creatures squatting there on his drive. At first he thought they were frogs because he had seen them hopping. He looked down at the girl who was also eyeing the creatures nervously.

"What's happened?" he said to her.

"Rats," she whispered, then she seemed to faint.

He looked back at the weird animals and was just in time to see them leap over his fence. He was stunned. Either he had imagined it, or two rats had just leaped over an eight foot high fence from, he judged, at least a dozen feet away.

"More like frogs," he said to himself. "Ones that bite, and bloody powerful."

Chapter Six

The nightmare about stinking, wet, horrible rats seemed to disappear into a distant haze, and as she was just waking, a beautiful dream took its place. A dream about walking along one of the beaches of Ibiza, naked as she had been much of the time on a recent holiday with her friend Tracey, only this time she was hand in hand with John Farrell.

She absolutely loved being out in the open, in the glare of the hot sunshine and, of course, *in puris naturalibus*. She knew that she had a beautiful body and worked hard to keep herself in good condition. She loved watching men's heads turning towards her as she walked past them on the beach, and laughed when, occasionally, a young lad who had probably never seen a completely nude girl in the flesh before, suddenly leapt out in front of her with a compact camera pointing at her, clicked the shutter button several times, then dashed off as though expecting her to chase him. She thought it rather sweet that the young boy would be back at school the following week showing off those pictures to all his friends. She was very self-conscious the first time she walked naked on the beach, though, but now it excited her, and she knew that her pubic hair glistened with the excitement of it. This made the men stare even more, and so this excited her more until, sometimes, she actually had an orgasm and she would have to lie down, breathless, on the sand. Then, of course, some men would rush forward to inquire if there was anything they could do for her. This had once given her the idea of being a stripper. She had not actually done it, as yet, but she often fantasised over the notion. She simply adored the way men looked at her, admiringly and longingly, so totally lost in their own little world of fantasy.

Now, it was early evening, the sunset was wonderful and, she had only just noticed, her man was also naked. His body was quite pale compared to hers which she was proud to admit was well toned as well as being quite tanned, but she smiled with deep satisfaction at him. He still looked lovely and she was incredibly happy.

"Let's go back to the hotel," she whispered, putting her arms around him and pressing her bare front up against his.

But he only laughed and told her to wake up. She felt disappointed that he didn't seem to be more keen. She wanted him to be more amorous but she could still feel his erect penis pushing against her.

"Come on, I know you want this body."

"I do, but I respect you too much."

Sue Sherringham woke up with a start and sat bolt upright.

"Where am I?"

John Farrell eased her back comfortably onto the settee and adjusted a pillow under her head.

"You're in my house, you're okay but you've had a bit of a shock - a sort of accident. By the way, thanks for the presents."

"Presents?"

"Rats? White rats? Rare Siberian rats?"

"Oh, Christ, rats!"

At that moment Sue became aware of the stiffness and stinging in the side of her face. She put her hand up and felt a soft bandage there, then noticed some dressing on her hand, too, as the strange memory of the day's events came flooding back to her.

"What happened?"

"I confess I've never seen anything quite like them," John told her. "I thought that they..." He broke off as she appeared to be listening for something... from outside.

"Is it still raining?" she asked.

"It's been like cats and dogs continuously for nearly three days now," John told her. "The forecast doesn't look good, roads are blocked, and so I'm afraid I've made the decision that you're staying the night here."

She looked at him, smiled and held his hand.

"Fine," she said.

John Farrell could not sleep. He was not sure whether it was because of the strange events which had led up to him not sleeping (or trying to sleep) on the settee, or simply because the settee itself was not designed for lying on. It was not the kind which unfolded into a double bed. He could hear the rain still falling as heavily as ever so that might also have had something to do with it. There was also the fact that in his bedroom, *in his bed*, there lay one of the most beautiful women he had ever set his eyes upon. But no. He shook his head and laughed. She had nothing to do with it. Momentarily, his thoughts returned to Kirstie, the girl he had first begun dating before his divorce. His feelings had developed so deeply, and so quickly, that now, with hindsight, he was not sure whether she had simply been the right girl at the right time, giving him the things he had desperately wanted like love, affection, and sex, or had he really loved her? He let out a hefty sigh. She had such a soft, warm, pleasant manner with a sweet, sexy voice. She had been precisely what the doctor ordered, but was it true love? Now what were his feelings about her, or about anybody, with that beautiful, young girl Sue now sleeping in his bed? He put his hand down inside his underpants and flicked at his penis to try and subdue the swelling. After that he could not resist a quick fiddle, but not actually what you could call a wank.

No, he told himself again. This is ridiculous. He tried to force thoughts of Sue out of his mind, and replaced them with less exciting ones. The rain. Yes that was boring. Those rats that Sue had bought. He hoped that Sam would like them. He decided to get up and check on Sam. He went into her bedroom and looked at her fast asleep. She, too, was beautiful and looked even more so when she was asleep. People had always told him that she took after him and was not at all like Lou, his ex-wife.

John Farrell and his former wife had not been a perfect match, and he had forgotten why he had actually married her in the first place. He supposed that she had seemed dependable enough and reasonably stable at the time, although the continual bickering and nagging did get him down. They had even argued horribly on their honeymoon, and divorce had actually been mentioned during that fortnight, but somehow they made their marriage last for nine years.

He pulled Sam's blankets up a little bit further and tucked her in so she looked more snug. Then the child murmured something, giggled in her sleep then rolled over, pulling all the blankets with her. John kissed her on the forehead, then left her room.

Just then he heard a cry - from his own bedroom. Sue needed tucking in, he thought with a grin. He went in to see her and switched the light on its dimmest setting.

Sue was sitting up in bed and leaning forward, her arms folded tightly over her bare breasts. She looked up at him.

"Christ," she croaked. "I feel bloody awful."

"Sue, I..."

John sat next to her, put his hand on her bare shoulder and instantly noticed how hot and clammy she felt. "Jesus, you're sweating."

At first she seemed to ignore him and went perfectly still, even holding her breath. Then she let out a long sigh.

"Oh, it seems to come and go. It's passed for now."

"What does?" John demanded urgently. "What comes and goes?"

"Pain," Sue whispered. "Pain in my chest, but it's gone now. I'm okay."

John put his arm round her and let her rest her head upon his chest. She was wet. He could feel her hair on his face, and even that felt clammy. Then he placed his other hand on the bed and was shocked to discover that it was soaking.

"Sue," he told her. "I'm calling a doctor right now."

At first he thought that she had gone back to sleep, but then she moved her head.

"Don't be silly," she said, still whispering. "I'm fine, but I must visit the bathroom."

"Okay, if you're sure."

John helped her out of bed. He had to suppress a gasp of excitement as the sheets fell away from her, but she appeared to be utterly oblivious to the fact that she was now standing in front of him completely naked, and when she was standing on the floor he still held onto her. But then she pushed him away.

"I told you, I'm fine," she snapped at him suddenly, as she made for the door. "Now, I'm sorry but just leave me to..."

"Okay, okay. I only wanted to..."

Sue Sherringham was in the doorway when she collapsed. John rushed forward, knelt down beside her and cradled her head in his arms.

"Sue!" he gasped. "Are you okay?"

"Of course I'm not bloody-well okay," she hissed breathlessly through gritted teeth. "I went dizzy, then fell arse over tit!"

"Look, I'm calling a doctor, no matter what you say."

He was both relieved and surprised when she responded with "Okay." He picked her up and placed her back onto the bed, then arranged the pillow so she was in a half sitting up position. She panted with her tongue hanging out.

"Right, now", he told her, "you stay here nice and quietly, be sensible, and I'll call Doctor Ulmilmahey. Now, that's a lady doctor, I've had her myself, well, in a manner of speaking, several times, and I've..."

He broke off suddenly as Sue's whole face contorted terribly in obvious agony and her whole body arched upwards at a grotesque angle.

"Ah, shit, shit, SHIT!" she screamed. "Ah, fucking hell!"

"What?" John yelled back at her, terrified.

"My..." She gritted her teeth. "... My arms."

"Arms?"

John noticed that her arms were tightly wrapped around her chest again as she doubled up bringing up her knees. As he rushed to the light switch, he thought he heard her utter, "Ah, my face," and it was only after he turned the light on full brightness that he saw how grey she looked, and her lips seemed blue.

"No, I don't believe this!"

He took her hand and felt for her pulse, and the fairly irregular beat made him realise his worst fears. He dashed to the telephone in the hallway, dialled 999, and when a lady's voice said: "Emergency Service - which service do you require?" he replied: "Ambulance please, and make it fast. Someone's having a heart attack."

When he arrived back in the bedroom, he was horrified to see her lying completely still. He checked for her pulse again, and when he realised there was no pulse, with tears welling up in his eyes, he saw at the same moment that she was no longer breathing.

He grabbed her with his hand at the back of her neck, treating her a little more roughly than he should have done for he now, was himself, in shock, then he pulled upwards so that her head was lying back. He pulled her chin down, took a deep breath, pressed his mouth tightly over hers and gave her four good breaths. He then knelt over her, put the heel of his right hand between her breasts, put his left hand over his right and gave her four vigorous chest compressions. He did this quite heavily because, despite his shocked state, he realised that the springiness of the bed would absorb some of the pressure and he did not want to waste time by moving her onto the floor. Feeling her pulse again he was relieved to feel that it was there. Faint, but it was back.

He decided, however, that she still required the mouth-to-mouth resuscitation. He took off his watch and, using the seconds hand, began to time the breaths he was giving her. He struggled to remember his first aid lessons from years ago. What was it? Two blows at a time, up to sixteen blows per minute. He started work, keeping a regular check on her pulse which was always there, but still very weak.

Ten minutes later, the ambulance arrived. Relieved, but absolutely exhausted, John let the ambulance men in. They brought in oxygen apparatus and a stretcher. John watched them take her, but he knew that it was he who had saved her life. He felt hot and cold at the same time. He felt like laughing and crying at the same instant, in fact, at that moment he felt like puking his guts up.

John Farrell went to the lavatory and sat in silence.

Chapter Seven

It was now two whole days since Alan Brynn and his mate, Desmond Prickett, had discovered Alan's empty cages with their wire fronts chewed open, a jagged hole gnawed through the shed door and, more to the point, the rats and the mutant frograts gone. The young men had followed Alan's idea of going round offering their services as rat catchers, only now they were doing it in desperation and not just to make an easy buck. As Alan admitted himself, he was not absolutely sure that his idea had been safe. He had not finished his experiments to ensure that the creatures wouldn't breed, but also, and perhaps more importantly, the offspring would not inherit the dreadful venomous traits of the yellow West Indian tree frog.

They were now out in Des's van, a little way from Alan's home in the countryside, and on a residential estate. As Des took a turning onto the main road, Alan noticed to his left, that there were plenty of open fields with the river running straight through. With the huge amount of rain they had been having lately, the water level looked hazardously high. It was still drizzling on and off, and the riverbanks were overflowing with water gushing over the pathways.

"Okay," he said loudly so that Des could hear him over the noise of the van's revving engine. "We'll try again here."

Des changed down a gear and began to slow down.

"All right. Let's do, say, one in every three houses. We'll start at the end, here we are..." he steered into the roadside and pointed "... number one, then you do number four, I'll do number seven, and so on."

"God, we should do every one to be sure," Alan replied anxiously.

"Well, neighbours do talk to each other and we've got to cover as large an area as possible." Des sighed as he pulled up the handbrake and switched off the engine. "Leave our names and telephone numbers as before."

As Alan released his seatbelt, Des suddenly caught him by the arm.

"Look Alan, what if those little bastards are poisonous, and what if they are breeding so we can't be sure if we've caught them all?"

Alan looked at him evenly.

"I told you, they can't breed because I gave the little ones an injection which is the equivalent of the pill - the effects of which are permanent."

"Okay, great, but what about the big mother?"

"What about it?"

"What do you think?" Des was exasperated. "Will it mate?"

"I injected it and treated it in a laboratory," Alan reminded him patiently. "But ordinarily I shouldn't think a rat is going to come along willingly to bonk a frog."

After a pause, Des said, "Listen, arsehole, what about the poison? What could the effects of that be?"

"I hadn't completed my tests," Alan admitted slowly. "I was pretty sure they were all right, and the mother was definitely rendered harmless, although I suppose the little ones could bite, but then again ordinary rats can bite. I'm afraid we won't know for certain until I recapture at least one to finish testing. But, I have to admit..." he paused for a moment, wondering whether to tell Des the full truth. "... if they have inherited the poison then it can be lethal."

Des' face went grey. "You mad lunatic," he breathed.

Alan looked away.

"At worst, if the victim is very old, or very young, the poison can kill. At best, the victim may suffer illness, could even have a heart attack, the severity and consequences of which would depend on the victim's age, fitness, and how quickly medical attention was obtained. But," he added, "I honestly don't think that anyone is going to come to any harm."

"Come on," Des said at last. "We've got work to do."

Des strode up the garden path of the first house which had a brightly polished brass No. 1 screwed to the old wooden front door, while Alan went straight to No. 4. Having knocked, after a very short moment a middle-aged man of thin build and a slightly greying beard, opened the door.

"Hi, man." He raised his right hand to his visitor.

"Hello, Sir," Des began politely. "My company are visiting this area and..."

"I'm not buying anything," the man told him assertively.

"No, Sir," Des said. "Quite right, and I'm not selling anything, but..."

"Then what?"

"Rats," Des blurted out. "We exterminate rats."

"No rats here," the man told him, fondling his beard. "But we seem to have a huge amount of frogs."

Des looked at him in disbelief. "Frogs. Jesus, I wonder."

"They're not dangerous are they? It must be something to do with the weather. The spawn gets washed up onto the paths, and the little critters take up residence in your garden. You know, I've got tadpoles swimming in the puddles in my back garden."

A horrible thought just entered Des's mind.

"Could I take a look?" he asked.

The man looked at him with a puzzled frown. Suddenly, there was an almighty bang from up the road. Des looked round and to his horror saw the figure of Alan Brynn lying down in the garden a few doors up, and next to him stood a man holding a shotgun.

"Christ!" Des shouted, already in full flight. "I'll be back."

Mark Hammond had been awake for over an hour, but had been unable to move. Extreme tiredness had made him try to return to his slumber, but a splitting headache had not allowed him the luxury. He had inadvertently left his curtains open in the middle and now the narrow ray of light made him grimace. He looked at his watch, 9:25 a.m.. He hadn't even phoned work to tell them he couldn't come in today. Not well.

He'd had a cold coming on for days, and now it looked as if it was going to take its toll. Those bloody inconsiderate, uncivilised neighbours of his had kept him awake until 1 a.m. with their loud music, banging and shouting. Well, this time they would pay. He had already spoken to Mr Smythe next door, and told him that if he wanted to be an uncivilised son of a bitch, then two could play at that game.

Mark struggled from his bed, wondering what to do about his rotten neighbours. He pulled on his pants, went to the bathroom, lifted the toilet seat and groaned. He'd done it again. He'd been for a number two in the middle of the night, but had forgotten to flush the bastard away. Just look at that bloody thing, he thought, staring up at him without expression, except that it was there, and there would be a similar one there tomorrow, and the next day, and the next, until he remembered to flush the bog at night.

He had a piss, flushed the toilet then opened the bathroom window to let out the foul whiff of the unflushed dump. He looked out onto his rear garden. Still drizzling. The grass and path were waterlogged giving the whole back yard a totally uliginous appearance. Then something else caught his eye. From his bathroom window, he could also clearly see into his neighbour's garden. And there, cleaning itself under the cover of some tree branches, was their fat, black cat.

Mark Hammond grinned wickedly to himself and, forgetting all about his splitting head, went back to his bedroom. He hurriedly finished dressing, then went to the bottom, right-hand drawer of his cabinet. Pushing socks and gloves out of the way, at the back he found it. Unused for some time now, was a fairly hefty air pistol. He grabbed it, then carried on scrabbling around until he found something else - a small round tin. He rattled the tin, then flicked the lid off, and was relieved to see he still had some ammo left. He estimated possibly about a hundred pellets. Great, he only needed a few, and these point-two-twos, from short range, must surely inflict the desired results.

Loading the single shot, break-action pistol, he went back to the bathroom, threw the window wide open, rested his elbows on the window ledge and steadied his right hand with his left. Then, glancing quickly up and down next door's garden to ensure no one was around, he smiled with satisfaction to see the cat still sitting there licking its paws. He took aim. He knew he was a good shot and couldn't miss from a distance he estimated to be about fifty feet.

He fired. Crack! Instantly the cat shrieked and leaped about six feet into the air. Hammond roared with laughter, then pulled the barrel down to reload. He popped in a pellet, flipped the barrel back up with a decisive click, then took aim again. The cat was still there, struggling around on its back, trying to bite at something on its side which told him where the first pellet had struck. He took careful aim, attempting to shoot it in the top of the head.

Crack! The cat spun over violently, then landed on its back with its legs sticking up in the air. But then Hammond was astonished to see it was still moving and screaming. He stopped laughing, for even he realised that it was time to show pity. He would have to finish it off humanely. Again, he reloaded.

But as he was taking aim this time, an astonishing sight met his eyes. Both his garden, and next door's, appeared to be swarming with frogs.

Then he heard someone knocking on the door.

That morning, as they did the drying and clearing up from the party the night before, Baldric Smythe and his wife, Doreen, were not speaking to each other. Doreen had called him an inconsiderate piece of scum, and he had retaliated by belting her one. He had caught her with the back of his hand on the side of the forehead, and at first he was concerned that the bruise might be enough to see him in a police cell for the day. But that morning, it hardly looked like anything at all, so now he was more worried about whether that idiot from next door, Mark Hammond, had heard anything. Once, a long time ago, Doreen had called the police after a fight. She had scratched his face and kicked him in the bollocks, and he, instinctively, had pushed her away, but had accidentally hit her head on the door frame. He had scratches on his face, and balls that felt like they were about to explode, and she didn't have a single mark or lump on her.

And the police had arrested *him*. A WPC, and a young policeman who was obviously new to the job, and even more obviously reluctant to arrest a man on the evidence of an ill-mannered, foul-mouthed old cow like Doreen, in total indecision, went next door to see if they had heard anything. Needless to say, Hammond's evidence went against Baldric. Eventually, however, he was allowed back home owing to a lack of reliable evidence.

Even so, Baldric Smythe didn't want evidence, for instance the say so of a neighbour, going against him in future. And, funnily enough, as querulous and neurotic as Doreen was, seemingly hating him one moment then needing him the next, the two of them did not really want to be separated with him in a police cell. They had a curious, love-hate, can't-live-with can't-live-without, relationship.

The party had gone on until quite late the night before, and everyone had got a bit pissed, but now he needed to sort things out before he went to work. He was already going to be late. He looked at the clock on the kitchen wall. 9:25 a.m.

"Look, Dor," he said. "I'm sorry, okay?"
No answer.
"I was a bit tired, a bit rat-arsed..."
"A bit?"
"Okay, a lot, but so were you."
Silent treatment again.
"I promise it won't happen again," Baldric said with feeling.
"You said that before," Doreen told him, looking up from the washing up, and looking through the window out onto their back garden.
"Yes, I know, but this time I really mean it, and..."
"Ah, look at old Soots, cleaning his paws."
Baldric smiled at the mention of the old cat. A change of subject normally meant that he was forgiven.
"Yup, he did pretty well for himself last night, and this morning. You know he polished off a whole..."
Suddenly, as they were watching, Soots screamed and jumped into the air. Then, as he landed, he began thrashing around.
"Jesus Christ!" shouted Baldric.
"What the fuck happened?" screeched Doreen.
"I don't know, it was like he was hit by something."
And as they watched, something else seemed to strike the cat.
"Oh, go to him," pleaded Doreen.
Baldric raced out of the house, now suspecting what had happened and where the pellet had come from. He did not go all the way out into the garden, but looked up until he saw an open window, and a hand holding a pistol pointing out of it. He strode back into the house failing to see an army of frogs advancing from the bottom of his garden.
"What's going on?" Doreen demanded.
"Shot!" Baldric told her. "The cat's been shot."
He went to the cabinet in the dining room where he kept his shotgun.

Alan Brynn knocked on the door at number four, and waited for about a minute, and then decided to knock again. The lazy bastard was probably still in bed, he thought, so he would give him a minute or two. He looked down the road and saw Des talking to some bearded Johnny. As he knocked for a third time he thought he heard some impatient voice calling, "All right, coming," then he distinctly heard feet on the stairs.

The door opened. There was a young man, probably mid-twenties, standing there. Alan's first impression was that he was just scruffy and unshaven, but the guy did not look well. Very pale, in fact. His shirt was hanging outside his jeans and, for some reason, in his right hand he was holding a pistol.

"Um," Alan began apprehensively, "I er... we're pest controllers, and we're in the area because a lot of people have reported having seen rats."

"Rats," the young man grinned. "Not frogs by any chance?"

"What?" Alan was completely taken aback.

Just then, another man's voice came hissing with hatred from the corner of the house.

"You cunt, you shot my fucking cat!"

And there was the most belligerent-looking individual that Alan Brynn had ever seen. A man, in his shirt sleeves and braces, pointing the twin-barrels of a shotgun right at him. Alan instinctively threw himself onto the ground, and a split second later the gun went off with a deafening roar. Alan only jarred himself slightly on the ground, and luckily for Hammond, the gun had been pointed directly upwards when fired, but this had the desired result. As Alan got up, he thought the young man was going to faint with shock.

Desmond Prickett then appeared breathlessly on the scene.

"What the..."

He saw Alan standing up, and brushing himself down.

"Thank God, I thought you'd been shot."

Baldric Smythe pointed the barrels of his shotgun into the face of Mark Hammond.

"He's the one who's gonna get shot. He just shot my cat."

"Oh, how uncivilised." Hammond was recovering, and he had the tenacious nerve to point his air pistol at Smythe. "I hate people who are uncivilised."

"Listen, sucker," Smythe hissed nastily. "That's an air pistol, and this is a shotgun. Compared to my weapon, you've got a pea shooter."

Open-mouthed, Des gazed disbelievingly at Smythe as he continued to point the gun at Hammond, and wondered at the obduracy of Hammond, pointing an air pistol into the menacing face of the obnoxious Baldric Smythe.

"I thought you said something about frogs," Alan said, partly to save one of these uncouth individuals from being shot.

"Frogs?" Des said. "That's what my man at number one was going on about."

He also hoped that if these undesirables were hell-bent on wreaking death and vengeance upon each other they would save it for another day.

"Now who the hell are you?" Smythe demanded.

"Why I'm Mr Prickett," Des informed him nicely, "and this is my partner..."

"Get out of my way. You've had it, Hammond." Smythe pointed the barrels of his shotgun again. "There's still one cartridge in there, and guess who's gonna get it?"

This fearful altercation was suddenly interrupted, and their attention was diverted as, just then, there was a dreadful scream from Smythe's back garden.

"Doreen!" Baldric Smythe exclaimed as he dashed off.

"You know, there's something strange going on round here," Des said to Alan.

"You don't know the half of it," Hammond told them, blowing out his cheeks with relief.

"Come on, let's see."

Alan led the way, and then Des and Mark Hammond followed the path round to Smythe's back garden.

They could not believe the sight which greeted them. The garden was swarming with frogs, and the noise of croaking defied description. Most were croaking - some were *squeaking*.

Then they saw Mrs Smythe, kneeling, holding a cat which was obviously dead.

"Frogs don't bite," Mr Smythe was saying. "I keep telling you, that bastard Hammond shot it with a point-two-two break-action air pistol."

"No, I saw them as Soots was trying to get up. They attacked him. Look, you can see where he's been bitten."

"I don't understand this," said Des. "These are just ordinary frogs. The only thing unusual about them is the vast number of them."

Alan stooped to pick one of the frogs up. He held it up and took a close look at it.

"You're right. I must admit, this is odd!"

"Listen, you silly cow," Smythe persisted. "Frogs do not bite!"

"There they are!" cried Mrs Smythe, insistently pointing.

"I can see them, they're all around, but they're..."

They all looked in the particular corner where Doreen Smythe was pointing, and there, in the corner, were the frograts. There were about a dozen, slightly larger than the ordinary frogs, and with heads like rats - and with teeth.

"Jesus, we've found them!" Alan whispered.

"Oh, my God!" yelled Des. "What do we do now?"

"What are they?" asked Hammond, bewildered by all of this.

"No time to explain," Alan whispered, gesturing to Hammond's air pistol. "Have you got much ammo?"

Hammond grinned and tapped the tin which was visible in his pocket.

"About a hundred pellets."

"Alright, good. Start shooting at them, as quickly as you can, but I want one alive."

But at that moment, Mr Smythe, having seen the mutants, discharged the second barrel of his shotgun at them. The upshot of this was that four of the creatures were just blown apart, but the others began hopping about madly, and scattered in all directions. Two of them went straight for Baldric Smythe, and as he turned to the house to get more cartridges, they landed on his back and bit into his neck. Smythe screamed in rage, dropped the shotgun and began batting at them with his hands. Three others went for his distraught wife who tried to run. She had to drop the dead cat to protect herself.

There were three others, hopping, croaking and squeaking at the same time.

"Quickly!" Alan told Hammond. "Start shooting!"

But Hammond was already taking aim. Crack!

"Got one," he laughed, as Alan and Des rushed to the assistance of the Smythe's. He hurriedly reloaded and took aim again as Des grabbed one of the horrible creatures from the inside of Doreen Smythe's right thigh. Des grimaced when he saw the huge chunk of meat it had torn from her. It was the first time he'd seen or touched one of the loathsome, hybrid creatures. It struggled in his grasp and snapped its teeth at him. God, it was horrible. A frog with a rat's skull, teeth - and bristly hair, too.

"Don't let it bite you," Alan yelled as he broke the neck of one of Mr Smythe's attackers. "Kill it quickly."

Its neck snapped easily in Des's fingers. He felt like vomiting, but then Mrs Smythe's screaming reminded him that there were still more to deal with.

There was another crack from Hammond's air pistol, followed by a derisive laugh.

"How many's that?" Alan shouted.

"Two. There's another one over there."

"Get it quickly, please."

Des picked up a stone and smashed the skull of the second frograt which was eating Mrs Smythe's toes, while she herself was trying to squeeze the life out of the other one. Meanwhile, Alan was tearing one away from Mr Smythe's ear. He then drowned the creature in a deep puddle.

Their screams and shouts had drawn the attention of some of the other residents, and as Hammond was taking aim at the last creature, he was aware of quite an audience who were horrified at the sight of millions of frogs hopping around, but even more horrified at the struggle which appeared to be going on with vile looking creatures which vaguely resembled frogs.

"Keep out of the way," Hammond yelled at them, then he fired. Crack! "Got the bastard!"

But suddenly finding himself with an audience had put him off at the most vital second. He'd scored a hit, but it wasn't a clean kill. The frograt was wounded, but he could still see it moving. He hurriedly reloaded but, as he looked up, he was just in time to see it hop right over a hedge more than twelve feet away, leaving one of its front legs behind. He hurried to the spot but it was gone.

"That last one got away," he shouted.

"Shit!" came a breathless reply.

"It's sure wounded, though. I've got a bit of it here."

"Okay," said Alan. "It'll probably die later, then."

There was now just one left - that was the one Doreen Smythe still held in her hands.

"We'll take that one alive," Alan shouted to Des.

Des nodded, strode over and tried to grab it from her, but in her shock she would not let go, so he had to give her a firm shove in the chest with his foot.

Then all at once, the other frogs, the ordinary ones, began to disperse. Croaking as they went, they began to make their way down the garden, and back towards the river. Alan decided to grab one. Maybe there was some clue connected to the other mutant creatures which could tell him how they had bred in such vast numbers.

As Baldric Smythe and his wife lay on the grass injured, the other residents who had witnessed the frightening scenes began to creep forward.

"What were they?" ventured one elderly lady.

"We don't rightly know," Alan lied, "but we're going to find out. Now, if we give you our number, we would ask you to contact us if you see these creatures again. In the meantime, would someone call an ambulance as there are two casualties."

They thanked Mark Hammond for his assistance, then took their struggling specimens back to the van. The frograt and the ordinary frog were each placed in a reinforced metal cage. Alan returned to the garden briefly to collect the dead frograts which had been shot, placed them in a black, plastic rubbish bag, then returned to the van, slinging them carelessly into the back.

Des got behind the wheel of the old van once again, and as Alan climbed in next to him, he caught the grave look of concern in the younger man's face.

"We're nearly home and dry now, right?" he queried hopefully.

"Not quite."

Alan slammed the door and fastened his seat belt.

"Okay, what's up?"

"Now we know what the infected mother rat can produce," Alan began slowly, "and don't forget she's still out there somewhere, and the tree frog..."

Des started the van and began to drive.

"I thought you said it was rendered harmless."

"I just want to be sure."

Des stared at him in wonder while the van continued to accelerate to forty miles per hour.

"You're not sure? Oh, well that's marvellous! Try to understand and accept for once in your life that what you've done is tantamount to the most grossly stupid act in the entire history of the universe."

"Look out, or you'll kill us!" Alan screamed suddenly.

Des had to break hard and swerve violently to avoid hitting an oncoming Triumph Herald - a very early 948cc model.

*

Beneath the old rotten fence, one of the hideous living things was getting hungry, but it still waited patiently. The other creature was no good to it any more. At first it had been warding off other creatures like large birds, adders and rats, but now it seemed to become aloof, and even threatening towards it. It was becoming more like one of its enemies which it had, for so long, protected it against.

It was getting afraid of the other creature which was changing shape and colour and it was growing.

Then quite suddenly, it became excited. It heard a loud, impatient, rapid sniffing and something else. The other creature had sensed it as well. A smell - the smell of blood.

Then both creatures saw it. The one surviving frograt, bleeding and missing a leg.

The other creature, the elder frograt, pounced on it, tore it apart, and began to eat it. Afterwards it approached the prone creature which still lay there, pushing some food in its direction. Then it lay on top of the wretched creature, moving vigorously back and forth.

Chapter Eight

>...Where did she go, I'm tired of waiting here for her,
>where can she be, she's not with me,
>Where did she go, what will I do,
>where did she run, run away from me...

The words from the song, written and performed originally by Debbie Harry (where of course it was a *he* who had run away) but performed this time by two guys called Kevin Leavy and Simon Lovelace (neither of whom David Conner had ever heard of) were repeated again and again on the radio. Conner sat there listening, with a tear glistening in his eye, for these were the very words that reminded him of his first real love, Kirstie Harris or, to be exact, the song reminded him of his first relationship with her and why she had disappeared out of his life.

Kirstie herself had gone on about their six-month relationship which had resulted in her having her third child, after which he had left her, but suffering from selective amnesia, she had conveniently forgotten their previous relationship, long before he had got married to his present wife. Things were getting bloody complicated, he mused.

He had originally gone out with her for a mere two and a half months, but he had fallen in love with her the moment she had first held his face between her hands and kissed him so tenderly. The first night they met. This was something she did often, and it felt so affectionate and loving but, in retrospect, was this something she did to all the lads? What about this John Farrell bloke - how did he feel about her? Had she led him to her bed and let him make love to her the way he had done? Had she then taken over and forced him into playing the submissive role, or had he willingly done anything to please her just to see those luscious tits just above his head bouncing up and down with the soft moans of 'Oh, oh, oh,' getting progressively louder?

Then, one night he took her out to dinner and looking across the table at her lovely, happy face, he realised that this was the girl he wanted to spend the rest of his life with.

He then told her that he loved her. She looked even happier, though he remembered being slightly disappointed that she did not say she loved him. They went back to her house, then straight to bed, where they made love in the most spectacular, unforgettable manner. He recalled actually laughing and coming, at the same moment imagining that he was on some kind of fairground ride where you've got to hold on for your very life. She knew how to make love. She made lovemaking fun. That was all he wanted, and he fell in love with her easily.

He had to leave early the following morning to go to work, so he got up, kissed her goodbye, then left.

And then she dumped him, as if that whole wonderful experience had meant nothing, and now he knew the reason. He had been climbing walls thinking about his woman with another man, but now John Farrell Esquire was going to pay for that, and for his broken arm which was still in a sling, and for his missing teeth.

The music on the radio was beginning to have the soothing affect of a *berceuse*, and he needed to stay awake, so David Conner switched off the radio silencing Kevin Leavy and Simon Lovelace still singing the same *leitmotif* about some old bird who had gone away. Then he opened the glove compartment and took out the explosive device that he had made. He opened the driver's door and cursed the rain which was still falling heavily but it was only after he had stepped clear of the car and closed the door that he saw in the light from the street lamps the creatures he had first seen outside Kirstie's house the week before.

The frograts attacked before he had a chance to think about quickly getting back into the car. Lots of the horrible frog-like creatures, with evil, grinning, rats' snouts, leaped onto him as he tried to run. He fell headlong into a muddy ditch, but mercifully he was spared being eaten alive. The bomb, which he had intended for John Farrell's car, was detonated on impact and went off with a dazzling flash of light and a deafening bang. The body of David Conner, along with about forty of the hideous little beasts, were all blown to bits.

Early the next day, John Farrell was striding into Ward 8a of the North Wing General Hospital carrying a bunch of roses. He spotted Sue in the corner of the ward sitting up in bed and wearing a pair of headphones. She had a very serious look of concentration on her face. He quietly walked to her bed, gently pulled the headphones away from her and sat down by her side. Then he lay the flowers on her lap. Her face instantly lit up, and she grasped the flowers, looked round at him and, to his great pleasure, she flung her arms around him and hugged him tightly.

"Oh, John!" She held him even more tightly. After several more seconds, she looked at him very closely and said quietly, "You saved my life. I know because the doctor told me."

Before John could respond she planted her lips, which where now very moist, tenderly on his, and began to kiss him. John realised he was defenceless, so he just held on to her, receiving and giving wet kisses, until they were interrupted by a quiet, but firm, voice.

"You're not to do anything that will excite you," said the young nurse. "Now how's your pulse?"

John grinned up at her.

"Oh, just hangin' on in there."

"Not yours!" smiled the nurse. "I've still got to check Miss Sherringham's pulse regularly, and I'm to make sure that she keeps quiet and doesn't jump about too much."

The nurse held Sue's wrist for a few seconds and looked at her watch.

"Um, a slightly quicker rate than last time," she commented with mock seriousness, "but I'll put that down to the way you suddenly grabbed her."

"It won't happen again." John held his hands up.

"I'll find a vase to put the flowers in," said the nurse.

"Thanks." John passed the roses to her.

The nurse smiled at them, and as she moved away, Sue held John's hand.

"Sorry for getting carried away, but I did want to thank you."

"That's okay, I was really worried about you."

"I just don't remember much about it."

"Don't try to remember," John told her. "While you're in here just relax."

"I remember you coming in to say goodnight, and I felt awful, like my whole body hurt, but then..."

"Like I said," John held a finger to her lips, "don't worry, just relax."

"I do remember one thing very clearly," she said suddenly. "Earlier on, those things like rats... the things that attacked me?"

John had been pondering over that himself, but then had wondered if he had just imagined how fast they were and how high they had jumped - a height of eight feet from a distance of at least twelve feet - but then the scratch that was still visible on Sue's face was not imaginary.

Sue continued: "John, what's going on? I heard it on the radio just before you arrived. A man and woman, not far from your house, were attacked in their own garden by strange rat-like creatures which hopped like frogs. It said that two Pest Control officers were there on the scene, and someone with a gun shot some of the creatures, but the two wounded people were brought here. They're here in this hospital."

"Here? Christ, I wonder if they're all right?"

"No." Sue was virtually in tears now. "The man's dead."

"Dead?"

"Heart attack."

Sue held on to him as she cried. John cuddled her gently and patted her.

"Try to forget about it now," John told her. "Just rest and I'll be right here."

"They both had heart attacks," she sobbed in his ear. "The woman survived but the man died this morning."

•

John continued to cuddle her until he was sure that she was asleep. He looked at the lovely features on her face which were relaxed now, and hoped that her attack had not caused any permanent attenuation to her heart. He had heard that in some cases the heart could be weakened, and prone to another attack if the person did not take things more leisurely, but in other instances the heart muscle would fully recover. He settled her back onto her pillow, tucked her in snugly, then bent forward and kissed her on the forehead.

He thought how beautiful she looked, lying there with her head turned slightly to one side, her cheek resting on the back of her hand,

and waves of blonde hair tumbling over her pillow. He bent forward and kissed her again – this time on her cheek.

"Goodbye, my daring," he whispered.

"Bye," she mumbled back, her eyes still closed.

"I thought you were asleep," he laughed softly.

"I am," she whispered with a smile. "Half asleep."

"I'll come back to see you tomorrow."

"What about this afternoon?"

"Can't I'm afraid," he sighed. "I'm collecting Sam from school."

"How is she?"

"She's fine, and I nearly forgot, she sends her thanks for the white rats. She loves them. I couldn't keep them as a secret until Sunday, but she still hasn't decided on names for them."

Sue smiled, nodded silently and let out a huge sigh. John wondered if she had dropped back off to sleep.

"Sam also wondered if you would like to come to her party," he continued.

"Love to." Sue opened her eyes, looked up at John and reached out for his hand. He held her hand, and sat down next to her again. "You called me darling," she said softly, smiling dreamily.

"Well, I... what I meant was," John started, not being able to concentrate on his words with her beautiful face looking up at him smiling so seductively.

"What was it you meant, my darling?" she said softly.

"Darling?"

"That's what people call each other all the time when they're in love."

"In love?"

John's head was spinning with confusion. Was this gorgeous creature telling him that she loved him?

There was a tender pause as she reached out for him again, put her lovely, soft, bare arms around his neck and pulled him towards her. As if in a romantic fantasy film, they gazed into each other's eyes. Looking into her eyes John felt as if he was willingly being swallowed up by a warm, blue sea. He realised that he wanted to be with her forever.

"I love you," she whispered in his ear, and only then did he realise that he had just fallen in love for the very first time. What he had taken for love before had been a very pleasant state of mind indeed, but this was utterly fantastic.

Next, he decided to get into bed with her. He looked around to make sure that no one was watching, then he very quickly got undressed, threw his clothes over a chair, and slid into bed next to her.

"What do you think you're doing?" she giggled excitedly.

"Don't worry," he croaked as he cuddled up next to her, and the feeling of their bare tummies and thighs touching, as she pulled her lacy nightdress right up, gave him a wonderful erection. They just couldn't help themselves. It was the sheer naughtiness of it all, and the thrill of the chance of being caught that first made them do it, and then made them enjoy this first complete love-making experience together all the more. He was soon on top of her and, now between her legs, thrusting, gently at first, but gradually going inside her a little more deeply than before with each thrust. Then the thrusts became quicker and more urgent. Sue began to cry out, but then slightly prematurely, with the excitement of it, he began to come, pumping his juices into her. She imagined that her whole body was being filled up with the warm fluid from his body.

"Please don't stop!" she shrieked.

But he wasn't going to stop. After his exquisite climax he continued to thrust until her orgasm sent a tidal wave of ecstasy through her whole body, and the sudden energy and power made her bounce violently in the hospital bed causing the springs to creak. As their bodies both jumped and jerked together, he had to hold on to her tightly for fear that he would fall out of this narrow contraption that the hospital staff called a bed.

Then gradually they began to calm down and, save for their heavy breathing, as they were returning to normal, they each experienced a new love developing, warm and mellifluous. John rested his face next to hers, but because they were so hot, he turned his face away from hers and allowed himself a few gulps of cooler air. Then he opened his eyes.

He realised they were being watched by the nurse, whose face went bright red when she realised that she had been seen. But John did not mind in the least. He turned his face back to Sue, and as she turned to him and opened her lovely, blue eyes, he kissed her lips.

"I adore you," he told her, and when the nurse had fully composed herself, still with a grin on her face, she returned the roses in a vase and placed them on Sue's bedside cabinet.

Over an hour later, John was still holding on to Sue as though he wanted to be permanently welded to her.

Chapter Nine

Peter Hargreaves and Walter Richmond stood facing each other, proudly inspecting each other's uniforms. Each silver button shone like a tiny mirror. The two elderly gentlemen took turns in brushing specks of dust off the other's uniform, thoroughly inspecting them at the same time.

"Tummy in, chest out," Peter said seriously. "This is like the old days now, you know."

"I'll show 'em at the parade tomorrow," Walter said in a voice which had become croaky over the years. "Ho, ho."

Peter coughed. "You know, I will too."

"That's what I just said, you old fool. We'll both show 'em."

"People say it's over fifty years since the end of the war," Peter went on in a mystified tone. "It's not so long as that."

"I was talking to Mum just the other day, saying those old shelters should be looked after."

"You daft old bird," chuckled Peter. "Your Mum's been in her grave nearly thirty years."

"You're going deaf in your old age," Waiter croaked. "I didn't say Mum, I said Tom."

"And who's he when he's at home?"

Walter stood there looking totally befuddled, then he began suddenly and excitedly: "Enemy aircraft overhead - enemy aircraft overhead..."

"Rear gunner to Skipper," Peter joined in, instantly taking up the situation - alert as he had been more than fifty years ago when he was a twenty-one-year-old Flight-Sergeant in the Royal Air Force.

"Skipper to Gunner," Walter held out his arms and began running around the lounge.

"Red-nosed bandits coming in from above on port side."

"What range, Gunner?"

"Ten thousand yards, about ten of the bastards."

"We're over our target, release bombs."
"Bandits closing in."
"Keep her steady."
"Rat-tat-tat-tat-tat-tat-tat-tat-tat-tat."
"Dive, dive, dive."
"Too late, we're hit, bail out."
"I can't, I'm stuck."
"Both port engines are on fire - controls are damaged."
"My turret's stuck - I can't move."
"Skipper to all crew members, bail out, that's an order, and remember to be nice to the Jerries if you're taken prisoner."
"Rear gunner to Skipper," Peter yelled. "Go without me. Save yourselves. Get out before she blows, for God's sake."
Walter climbed across the settee and grabbed hold of Peter's arm.
"If we go, we go together, now try to get hold of..."
At that moment, Walter's wife walked in.
"What in heaven's name do you think you're trying to do?" she screeched in alarm.
"Don't get in the way, woman," Waiter croaked. "Can't you see I'm trying to save Peter from..." Then he stopped. He realised that he was not crawling along the floor of the stricken Lancaster Bomber, but walking across Peter's settee in his polished shoes. As Walter's wife began to laugh, he got down off the settee and Peter went to steady him. They held on to each other's arms. Grey, watery, old eyes gazed. Memories, as they had done thousands of times before, flooded back until there were tears. Tears of joy, tears of sadness, and tears of sheer, bloody relief.
"Fifty years, my God," Waiter coughed.
"Only for the people who weren't there, my old friend," Peter told him. "Something terrible happened fifty years ago. But for us it will never end."
Walter's wife abruptly stopped laughing. She was in her seventies but had a pretty good memory. She stood between the two old heroes and put an arm round each of them.
"Come on lads, put those suits away for tomorrow, then come down for your dinner."

The men were upstairs changing their clothes, while their wives, Valerie Hargreaves and Patricia Richmond were in the kitchen preparing the roast dinner which they would normally have had on a Sunday.

Although the weather was warming up, it had been wet again that morning and all the windows had been kept closed, but with the steam building up in the kitchen, Valerie decided to open some of the windows.

Valerie and Patricia had been close friends for over sixty years, and had met the boys, Peter and Walter, during the war. They had started to go out as a foursome when they were all on leave, and the great thing was that there had never been any misunderstanding about who should go with whom. Peter just clicked with Valerie, while precisely the same thing happened between Walter and Patricia. Then after the war they had a double wedding at the Church Of St. Patrick in Bedford.

The special war service to commemorate VE Day, (Victory in Europe) and the fiftieth anniversary of the conflict's end, was to be the following day, but the Hargreaves' and Richmond's were now having one of their quite regular get-togethers, and they were expecting three more guests who were due any minute. The Hargreaves' daughter, Hilda, her husband, Philip, and their seventeen-year-old daughter, Norma.

"Not like Hilda to be late," Valerie said, checking on the roast potatoes.

Patricia looked at the clock on the kitchen wall. Quarter past one, but just then she heard a car pulling into the drive. She looked out of the side window.

"They're here," she announced excitedly, "and, I don't believe it, another new car."

Valerie came to the window, saw her grand-daughter, Norma, waving, and waved back.

"Well, at least they're here, and not before time," she told Patricia. Then, going to the cooker, she opened the oven, pulled out the roast, placed it on the counter, and carefully made sure that everything was switched off.

"Right, I'll let them in - you go and check on the menfolk upstairs."

"Right then."

Patricia went off upstairs, knowing that she'd find Walt and Pete in the middle of reliving another bomb raid which had happened more than fifty years ago.

Valerie went to open the door.

"Not another new car, Philip?"

"You've got to get one of these, Gran," Norma enthused. "It's got air-conditioning, heated wing mirrors and, get this, come over here and look."

Valerie Hargreaves found herself being dragged into the car and virtually forced to sit down on the back seat.

"Look," she said, "this is very comfy and I'll be glad to sit here with you later, but the roast is ready."

"Never mind, Gran," Norma told her while Hilda and Philip stood there laughing. "This wont take a minute, you'll see."

"Hey, there's something not quite right with this."

Valerie was getting worried.

"This seat is becoming quite warm."

"Heated seats," Norma explained, "to keep your bum warm on cold frosty mornings."

"Well, I've never heard of such a thing." Valerie got out of the car and struggled to her feet. "When I was your age I was lucky if I had a second-hand bicycle to ride, and you're being chauffeur-driven around in a car with heated seats. Now come on, in you go. Dinner's getting cold."

During that three-minute period, while Patricia Richmond was upstairs helping the men to get ready for dinner, and Valerie Hargreaves was outside admiring Philip's new car, something very strange happened.

The frogs came along up the rear garden path completely unnoticed, then through the patio door which had been left ajar. They were being led by one that seemed far more intelligent than themselves. They did not know why they followed, they just did. They felt compelled to do so.

The creature that led the way was larger than the ordinary frogs, and was a much lighter colour with yellow, orange and green markings. It behaved differently to ordinary frogs and it was attracted by a mixture of different smells, but as the frogs arrived with the great yellow one in the lead, there was also something about the food which they found repelling. It was hot with fumes and vapour rising off it, and this the frogs' small brains were unable to comprehend.

As the smaller frogs hopped about on the smooth tiled kitchen floor, croaking at each other in confusion, the larger frog hopped up onto the counter where the roast was steaming, turned away from it as if sniffing the air, manoeuvred itself into a squatting position, and squirted something all over the cooked bird. Afterwards, the yellow West Indian tree frog, one of the two specimens discovered by Alan Brynn's uncle nearly two months earlier, hopped back down onto the floor, made a shrill sound at the other frogs, then led the way out again, hopping through the patio door and down the garden path.

By the time Valerie had returned to the house, the frogs were gone, and when the Hargreaves' and the Richmond's settled down to their dinner, no one noticed anything unusual.

And there were no complaints about the taste of the roast chicken.

Chapter Ten

Desmond Prickett woke from his nightmare with a violent start, then lay there on his back, breathless and sweating profusely. He was trying to remember what it had all been about, when he became aware of the thing which had woken him up. The telephone on his bedside cabinet was still ringing.

Des looked at the brightly-lit figures on his clock-radio. Nearly two. He answered the phone.

"Who the hell's this?"

"Des, it's me, Alan."

"Do you know what the time is?" Des demanded.

"Sorry, my old buddy. I think we are in serious shit."

"How come?"

"Man, get here right now. I've got to show you this."

Des paused for a moment while rubbing his forehead.

"Okay, but what's it all about?"

"The frograts. I require your expert analysis."

"Oh God! I thought that was all over."

"I'd hoped that it was," said Alan, "but somehow I don't think so. Just get over here."

"Well, I'll just get my trousers on, then..."

Des looked crossly at his telephone receiver.

Alan Brynn had already hung up.

Twenty minutes later Des was pulling the van into Alan's drive. He climbed out, tried to close the door without making too much noise, and was locking it when Alan suddenly appeared from the front of the house. Alan closed the door behind him, and began making his way down the path towards the shed.

"What's the problem?" Des called quietly, so as not to wake the neighbours.

"I'll show you!"

Des shrugged, and followed his mate down to the garden shed. Alan opened the door, stepped inside and switched on a lamp which was hanging from the inside of the old wooden roof. Des stepped in behind him, and then his jaw dropped wide open, and he felt sick.

All around the shed were shelves, and on the shelves were cages, in juxtaposition, and all with reinforced wire so that the occupants could not chew their way out. The 'occupants' were the most horrid, vile, living creatures that Des had ever seen. They were all unmistakably frogs but with rats' heads. Some looked more like frogs than others, but still had some bristly hair around their necks. They made croaking noises, and they tried to hop inside the confinement of their prisons. But others resembled rats more closely, and these made high-pitched squealing noises at the sudden sight of the two intruders. Des could see their teeth as they snarled menacingly. Drool oozed out onto the floor of the cages. He also noticed that these repulsive hybrid monsters were a fair bit larger than those killed the other day in the Smythe's back garden. The largest was almost a foot long. In all there were twenty cages - one creature per cage.

"Jeez, you found more of them," Des said at last.

"No," Alan told him assertively. "These are new ones."

Des looked at him as if he were a stranger.

"These", Alan continued, gesturing at the creatures, "were born on Monday night. The one we took alive the other day made a really disgusting mess in its cage. There was all this grey and green gunge everywhere, and before I knew what was happening, the cage was full of... well, at first they just looked like ordinary baby mice or rats."

"Okay, so the babies are..."

"I took each of the babies and put them in separate cages."

"Slow down a minute," said Des. "Am I missing something here, or are you telling me that the rat-creature you caught had babies, and these are the babies?"

"You've nearly got it," Alan nodded, "but I'm afraid our problem is a whole lot worse than that."

"Jesus H. Christ!" Des slowly took another look around the shed. Some of the mutants stared back, each one an unholy burlesque, something which should never have been permitted life. One of them actually began making a hateful hissing sound - its tongue lolled out and its eyes were like yellow slits in the light of the lamp. "How could things be worse than that?"

"These animals represent two litters," Alan told him. "Not one!"

"Oh what?"

"Yesterday morning, when I discovered the first eight babies, I put them in separate cages, then began to run more tests on the mother. Then I discovered that she was about to have more. Meanwhile, the first lot were growing fast and they haven't even been fed. I put the original one back in a cage on its own, and by this morning, they were the same size as their mother - one or two were even bigger."

Des took a closer look at one of the creatures.

"Now they're all bigger than the original," he remarked dryly.

"And the mother's cage was full of more babies - another twelve," Alan went on, gesturing at two levels of shelves at the far end of the shed. "That's that lot."

"Bloody hell!" Des realised that it was the second lot that mostly resembled rats, having more bristly hair. "And they're nearly the same size already, so what's it been mating with?"

"Itself," Alan concluded. "These creatures don't actually need to mate with anything. One of these loathsome monsters possesses both male and female reproductive organs, but I introduced a new strain, first with a yellow West Indian tree frog, then a rat, and then an offspring from those two. After that I'm afraid I've lost track of exactly what has happened."

"Okay, Doctor Brynn," Des groaned. "Why not concoct your own chimera and be done with it?"

Alan just gazed, open-mouthed.

"Oh, never mind." Des let out a hefty sigh. "Is there anything else you wish to say, my son?"

"Yes." Alan Brynn stood there like a dumbfounded mad professor who now looked more than a little apologetic.

"Oh, hit me."

"That's not it," Alan said with a sigh and a shrug of resipiscence. "She's going to have more."

"This is just a nightmare," Des looked at the inside of the old wooden roof. "I'll wake up in a minute."

"Look at her abdomen," Alan pointed excitedly. "What do you think's wrong with her? Chronic diarrhoea?"

Des peered closely at the revolting thing.

"She does look a bit swollen," he admitted, but when he looked up at Alan, he saw someone who looked really afraid of what he'd done.

He placed a hand on his friend's shoulder. "We'll think of something."

"For some reason I don't understand, their whole metabolism seems to have been accelerated."

"We'll kill them - all - here and now," Des told him.

Alan just stood there. He was beginning to tremble.

"We'll be done with it once and for all," Des added quietly.

"I don't think so." Alan's voice was shaky. "There could have been others born before we killed those the other day."

"We'll just have to hope," Des told him sternly. "Now, what about the other tests?"

Alan looked at him.

"Their bites are poisonous. The poison effects the victim's heart, but their urine is just as bad."

"Urine?"

"The tree frog squirts its poison which contaminates water, but they can squirt it as a defence, causing the victim, for instance a small mammal, to go into a trance, allowing the frog to escape. It uses the same poison on insects in the same way that some snakes hypnotise their prey. What I've created is a creature which bites and urinates like a rat, but now has the venomous trait of the West Indian tree frog. I've been reading up on this, and I've found that the tree frogs' poison contains a horrible acid which causes the victim to hallucinate and go totally mad before a larger animal comes along, kills it as an easy picking, and eats it."

Des could feel the bile suddenly rise up in his throat, but then there was a high-pitched, croaky squeal from the original frograt. Des and Alan peered closely at it as it rolled onto its side, and they could plainly see what looked like a mixture of frogspawn and bristles coming out of its rear.

"Right, that's it," Des growled suddenly at Alan, grabbing him by the arm. "What we have here is a real problem, and we've got to stop it right now before it gets bigger than the both of us."

He dragged Alan out of the shed, then left him standing there while he returned momentarily to his van. As he strode briskly back down the path, in the shadows of light coming from the shed Alan saw that Des was carrying a petrol container.

"What do you think you're doing?" Alan demanded.

"You started this nightmare," Des said in a steady voice, "and now I'm going to finish it. I'm going to destroy this whole caboodle. And, in any case, it's an old shed."

Alan knew what Des was planning, but realised that this was the best way. The shed was nowhere near anyone's house, and he had firefighting equipment in the hallway of his own house which he would use if any burning debris drifted unsafely.

Des went into the shed and immediately began throwing petrol everywhere, including over the terrified frograts. One last glance in the cage where the breeding frograt lay confirmed his worst fears - as he stood there more frograts were being born. He drenched them all, then poured the remainder of the inflammable liquid all over the floor. Then, standing in the doorway, he saw Alan standing there.

"Ready?"

"Right."

Alan began backing away as Des fished in his pocket for the matches. Des struck one, and as it flared in his hand, Alan was already in full flight up the garden path. Des threw the match, then instantly began running himself. He was hardly halfway up the path when the whole garden seemed to light up. There was a fairly loud whoosh, and hot air gusted in their direction. For a short time after that, they could hear sickening little squeals of agony above the crackling of the burning wood, but in a surprisingly short space of time, the fury of the fire, and the noise, began to die down.

Then they heard a voice from the darkness.

"Hey, fire in someone's garden. Call the fire brigade."

"We had better tell them it's all right," Alan told Des.

"No. Let them call the fire brigade. You've just woken up."

"Oh, right. I don't know anything about how it started."

"Vandals," Des suggested, watching the fire as it continued to die down.

Alan looked at him and smiled.

"Bloody vandals."

At that, Des just gazed up at the black, night sky as if hoping, or even expecting, that the stars would offer them some kind of thaumaturgic amelioration.

Chapter Eleven

Walter Richmond and Peter Hargreaves sat next to each other in the cockpit of the Lancaster bomber. Walter was muttering into the intercom while Peter was checking the rest of the instruments. Then Peter Hargreaves stood up, but had to stoop slightly to avoid bashing his head. He looked at his watch. It was nearly midnight.

"Time to go back," he gestured towards the rear of the aircraft. Walter nodded but didn't look up.

"Nearly time, gentlemen," he said softly into the mouthpiece of his headset. "Fuel on, starting engines now, weather report over sea is okay. Check your pressures, Flight Engineer."

Peter looked out of a side window on his way to the rear turret, and there were the two ladies, Valerie and Patricia, waving and blowing kisses. Valerie seemed to be trying to say something. Peter held his hand behind his ear and tried to lip-read. Confusing, the message appeared to be: "Is everything all right?" and: "Are you okay?"

He nodded, waved again, but as he continued on his way towards the rear turret, he heard a voice.

"I can't bear all of this. I'm going. I'll walk home."

The voice seemed familiar, but it was a very young voice - almost childish. He continued on his way to the turret.

As he climbed into his turret, he heard more voices, but tiny, distant and crackling sounds this time. He harnessed himself in and tested all the levers turning the cramped contraption round and manoeuvring the four guns up and down. Placing on his headset, he then pressed the little button next to the left earpiece.

"Rear gunner ready," he announced.

"Where the hell have you been?" Walter's voice roared.

"Sorry skipper, just saying goodbye to the women."

"You've got to forget them. This is the job in hand, so if you're quite ready, we're off."

Peter's heart thumped uncomfortably as the four Rolls Royce engines roared and the heavy aeroplane began trundling along the runway. As they taxied, Peter heard Walter's voice again.

"Squadron Leader to all aircraft. Remember the drill, stick together, and no radio contact once we're over the sea. Test guns at six thousand feet."

The noise from the engines died down, then the plane swung round causing Peter to shift uncomfortably in his turret. Then the engines roared again, and he felt unnerved, as he always did, while looking out of the rear as the aircraft accelerated forwards. This feeling, however, was quickly replaced by sheer exhilaration and excitement as the big, black bomber became airborne, and ascended into the night.

"Where were you born?" The SS officer's voice was quiet, almost friendly.

"England."

Peter tried to open his eyes, but turned his head away sharply because of the bright light.

"Yes, but where in England?"

"Pratt's Bottom."

"And where did you train to become a spy?"

"I'm not a spy," Peter said impatiently. "I'm Fight Sergeant Peter Hargreaves, No. FS3197, in the Royal Air Force."

"What are you doing here? What are your orders?"

"I was in a Lancaster Bomber. We were shot down, and I parachuted, then..."

"Who's we? Where are your crew members?"

"I don't know." Peter was confused now. "I really don't."

"So what do you want? Wein, weib und gesang?"

"The mission was to..."

"We shoot spies here," the SS officer snarled, "and you will be shot."

"I'm not a fucking spy!" Peter screamed.

"So, I'm listening. Where is your uniform?"

Peter lay in silence for a moment, still trying to open his eyes. Then he said: "Upstairs, in the cupboard."

The doctor shone a torch into Peter Hargreaves eyes and noticed no pupil reaction.

"We may have a case of crapulence here." He looked round towards Valerie Hargreaves. "When did he go like this?"

"He was fine," she murmured. "He did seem tired. We were having dinner, then he went to sleep in his armchair which is not at all unusual. Then he woke up halfway through the afternoon and, for some reason, became very angry. Mr Richmond was still there and..." she broke off, weeping.

"Then what happened?" asked the doctor kindly.

"I'm sorry," Valerie wailed. "I just can't believe it. Peter and Walter, and myself and Walter's wife, have been the closest and dearest of friends for over sixty years."

"I know."

"But then, Peter and Walter began arguing angrily then..."

"And then?"

"We couldn't believe it, but they started fighting, at their age. Before we could stop them, Peter punched Walter so hard, that he tripped and struck his head on the hearth tiles. We saw blood on him and called the ambulance."

The doctor put a comforting arm around Valerie Hargreaves.

"I can't believe he's gone," Valerie cried. "Poor Walt."

"Then what?"

"Peter just laughed and marched outside and he was..."

"What did he do outside?" asked the doctor.

Valerie blew her nose noisily.

"Danced. He was just there, dancing!"

They were at six thousand feet, and approaching the coast.

"Squadron Leader to all gunners," Walter's voice crackled over the intercom. "Test guns now."

Peter Hargreaves pushed the red button which was situated on the top of his right-hand control bar, and fired in rapid, short bursts, then he pulled the bar to the right, and the turret swung round. He eased the guns up and down, then swung the turret back to the left while continuing to fire. He stopped firing after a few seconds not wishing to waste too much ammunition, but he could still hear firing in the distance above the drone of engines, as gunners in nearby bombers were continuing to test their guns. After a short while, though, they had all finished testing, and Hargreaves heard the Squadron Leader's voice again.

"All right, chaps. Well done. No more radio contact until we're nearly over the target. I'll give the word."

Then there was a click, and silence apart from the steady, monotonous drone of the aeroplanes' engines.

It was approximately three quarters of an hour later when the whole sky lit up. They were over German-occupied territory, and powerful lights and exploding anti-aircraft shells were illuminating all around them like a spectacular firework display. And then Peter Hargreaves saw the first of the enemy fighters - a large squadron of Focke-Wolf 190's.

"Rear gunner to pilot," he yelled. "Enemy aircraft, starboard, five thousand yards."

"Break," came the command from Richmond. There was a terrific roar of engines as they increased power. The aircraft at the front of the formation dived while those at the sides banked and swooped in opposite directions.

There was an angry chatter of machine gun fire as British bombers and German fighter planes fired at each other. As the bombers levelled out, Peter Hargreaves saw one of the fighters coming straight for him, now at about a thousand yards and easily catching up with the Lancaster. He got it in his sights, judged the speed, distance and direction of the enemy, then fired. Almost simultaneously it began firing back, but at that moment Hargreaves saw its front end begin to glow. Then suddenly it disintegrated with a boom.

Through the ensuing cloud of black smoke came another fighter, a little further over to the right. Then the sound of more machine-gun fire, this time from one of the other bombers. Hargreaves was just taking aim so as to join in with firing upon the German aircraft, when his turret appeared to jolt. It twisted to the left. Hargreaves tried to move it back but it was jammed, and the bomber went into a steep dive.

"We're hit," came Walter Richmond's voice. "Everyone out."

Hargreaves tried to get out, but with the turret jammed in its present position, he couldn't budge.

"I can't, I'm stuck!" he screamed.

"I'm coming," Richmond shouted. "Everyone else, out!"

Hargreaves heard the other five men yelling at each other, then watched as, one by one, they bailed out. Then Richmond was crouching next to him, and trying to move the manually-operated controls of the turret, trying to wind it round to give him more room to climb through. At last the turret jolted suddenly and twisted back to its central position. The heavy bomber was in a terribly steep dive and they both knew that there was not much time left. They jumped, or rather, fell, out of the hatch which was right next to the turret.

There was no time to be scared. Hargreaves just gritted his teeth and closed his eyes as he felt icy air biting his face, and pushing and piercing his body as though he was naked. He heard the rising pitch of the bomber's screaming engines gradually fade away before a distant bang, but there were so many flashes of light all over the sky, and from below, that he soon felt totally disorientated. He'd been through the drill hundreds of times before, but this was the first time he'd experienced the situation for real, and mercifully he remembered to pull the ripcord. For a spit second he panicked, but then felt a sharp tug on his upper body, and at first it felt like he was actually going back up again.

Below him all he could see was clouds of smoke. He closed his eyes again, gritted his teeth and bent his legs slightly in anticipation before landing in a thankfully soft field. It could only have been a minute or so since he had escaped from the stricken Lancaster, and he knew that he had only just got out in time. Another split second and it would have been too late to use the parachutes.

He realised that he owed his life to Walter Richmond, and hoped that his friend had also landed safely. Apart from the occasional flash of light from the battle raging from up above, he was in total darkness, and was reluctant to call out for fear of attracting the attention of any enemy soldiers.

He began to gather up his parachute, preparing to bury it somewhere, but then gasped and held his breath when he thought he heard a distant shout.

His worst fears were realised as the beams of light from several torches were turned on in his direction, and harsh voices calling "Halt, allied schweinhund scheist," "Achtung, spion, hande hoch!" and "Nein, so was, meine kleine English mann," reached his ears.

He did not try to run. There was no point. He would have been dead within three seconds. He just stood there.

"Hande hoch!"

He put his hands up. "I am unarmed."

"Spion!" came another aggressive shout.

"No," he replied. "I am an officer of the Royal Air Force."

The German soldiers were very close now, and in the light of the torches which some of them carried, he saw that there were about eight soldiers, and at least three of them were carrying rifles. They were now about twenty yards away. Again he wondered where his pilot and the other crew members were.

"So," snarled one of the soldiers, gradually, getting closer, "where is your Air Force uniform?"

It was only then that Peter Hargreaves realised that he was wearing ordinary civilian clothes. He started panicking. This could not really be happening. He must have knocked himself unconscious when he landed, and this was just a frightening dream. But the barrel of a rifle was rammed painfully against his face, just under his nose. The pain was not imaginary.

"You are a British spy," snarled the German. "And so, accordingly you will be shot."

The doctor put a comforting arm around Valerie Hargreaves.

"I can't believe he's gone," Valerie cried. "Poor Walt."

"Then what?"

"Peter just laughed and marched outside and he was..."

"What did he do outside?" asked the doctor.

Valerie blew her nose noisily.

"Danced. He was just there, dancing"

But then, totally unexpectedly, Peter Hargreaves sat up on the bed. His eyes were wild and rolling back so that only the whites were showing.

"Valerie," he screamed in a coarse, deep throated tone that the elderly lady had never heard before. "Please help me. They're going to shoot me!"

Shocked, Valerie quickly scanned the room until her eyes fell on a small pair of scissors which were used for cutting some bandages. She ran to the table and picked them up as the doctor was turning to the door and calling for assistance, but before anyone could stop her, Valerie Hargreaves, seventy-three years old, rushed at the doctor and plunged the scissors deep into the back of his neck.

Chapter Twelve

Norma Richmond smiled seductively. The scene was very unusual, but she was excited like she had never been before. The smile, with loads of lip gloss, together with her other make-up, was at herself, for she stood in front of a large, full-length mirror. Her long, dark, wavy hair, she held in a bunch above her head as she began to tie it, and as she did this she leaned her body over to one side and, for the first time, began to admire her hips and the other womanly curves of her body, because as she stood there she was completely naked.

At seventeen, Norma had never considered herself attractive, and while other girls in her class at school were always discussing their boyfriends, she could never really understand the necessity of this and always felt far more interested in school studies and determined to do well in her exams. Some of her friends had even intimated that maybe she was just a late developer, and possibly a bit backward, although her exam results, so far, had proved that there was nothing wrong with her intellectually.

After discussing this matter fully with her parents, they assured her that there was nothing wrong, and in their opinion seventeen was still far too young to be fretting over boys. She went nearly everywhere with her parents, including on holiday, but that weekend she had begun to feel fed up with being molly-coddled by them the whole time.

In fact she'd had a terrible day. She'd gone with her parents to see her grandparents, because there was going to be some sort of get-together for the old grandpas, something to do with the war. They'd had dinner, then everyone's mood seemed to change, and the two old granddads had begun to argue about nonsensical things. In the end she'd told them that she couldn't bear all this nonsense, and had left, having to walk the three miles home.

Actually she had enjoyed the walk. It had given her time to think about herself, and she started to have ideas about experimenting with clothes and make-up. Actually, she had not got much in the way of clothes, not the sort that she wanted to try, but she knew of quite a few girls who could help her, and who could possibly lend her a sexy little party frock until she was able to get some of her own. As for make-up, her mother used some occasionally, and once bought some really deep red lip-gloss to wear at a fancy dress party. With a sexy grin she decided to try it, and began to feel the first longings for a man to behave utterly lasciviously over her.

When she had finally arrived home from Granddad's house, she went upstairs to her parents' room and looked at herself in the full-length mirror. What had been wrong with her all this time? Her hair just hung loosely with no style, her sloppy pullover was a shade duller than her unfashionable blue skirt, and her shoes would not have looked out of place on a boy.

She immediately stripped off and went to the bathroom where she washed her hair, spent some time putting in some of her mother's curlers, then got into the bath using loads of bubble bath - again from her mother's cabinet.

In the delightfully warm, slippery, soapy sea of bubbles she began to have feelings that she had never experienced before. She held her arms up behind her and threw her head back and lay in the bath with a look of abandonment. She felt what was like a moving feeling in her lower body, then her arms flopped tenderly around her as she cuddled herself, and her right hand moved slightly so that her fingers rested on the soft mound of dark hair between her legs. Instinctively, she began to masturbate. Then she started to squirm and thrash about in the soapy bubbles. When she climaxed she cried out, and by the time she'd finished, lying there breathless, there were as many bubbles on the bathroom floor as there were remaining in the bath.

Eventually, she climbed out of the bath, nearly slipped on the floor, then laughing, began to dry herself. She went back to the bedroom, sat on the edge of her parents' bed in front of the mirror, and began drying her hair, still in curlers, with the hairdryer. Then she started to try on some make-up - eyeliner and eyeshadow first, followed by some blusher on her cheeks, then the deep red lip gloss.

It was then that she realised what a beautiful girl she was and, standing there, still naked, began to smile seductively at herself in the mirror, and to cavort and wriggle around, admiring herself, like an erotic dancer. She took her hair out of the curlers, brushed it, then tied it into a bunch on top of her head, and leaning to one side, admired her hips and the other curvaceous aspects of her body.

With a sigh, she decided it was time to get dressed, so she went back to her own bedroom, opened her wardrobe and, with another hefty sigh, realised that she possessed nothing that she really felt like wearing. She took out a pale blue dress with floral patterns, considered altering it with a pair of scissors, but then finally decided that such a task would take too long and slipped it on over her naked body. She found a pair of her mother's high heeled shoes that fitted her, and went downstairs to make a telephone call.

In the telephone book she found the name she had thought of while lying there in the bath. Davey. Celia Davey was a girl from school. She was not particularly a best friend but she was okay and, more importantly, about the same size as herself. She was also remembered for daring to wear some of the most eye catching, revealing garments at parties. Norma just hoped that the girl was in, and could help her out that evening by lending her a really sexy dress to knock the lads' eyeballs out with.

She tapped out Celia's number. She heard the telephone ringing and after half a dozen beeps it was answered. It was Celia's mother.

"It's Norma. Is Celia there, please?"

"She's here," came the answer. "Hang on."

With relief Norma blew her cheeks out at the ceiling.

"Yeah, hi," Celia's voice at last.

"I want to ask a favour," Norma explained.

"Well, well, well," came a soft laugh. "And what could I possibly do for prim little Rosie?"

"Listen, Celia," said Norma with a mixture of exasperation but, at the same time, relief. "I'm not prim and proper, that's just an act to fool you all. Seems I sure fooled the lot of you."

"I don't believe it."

"I'll prove it, but I do need to borrow a dress off you for the party tonight. If you remember some time ago, you said you could lend me a dress if I needed one."

"I was joking."

Norma grimaced.

"Please?"

There was a pause, and at first Norma thought that Celia had hung up.

"All right, party girl," Celia chuckled at last, "but seeing that you're really such a party animal, why don't you wear one of your own many fine dresses?"

"I would," Norma replied quietly, "but my best one's been totally ruined in the wash. My mum went and put some old pair of my dad's blue and red socks in the same wash, and now the dress looks like the Union Jack."

"Sure thing," Celia said in a disbelieving voice. "I've got some outfits which you can try."

"Oh, great," said a very relieved Norma. "You're a real mate."

"Come right over."

With a very vague thought in the back of her mind wondering why her parents weren't home yet, Norma Richmond, wearing only a thin, blue dress and a pair of high-heeled shoes, went out of the front of her parents' house, and slammed the door behind her.

She never returned.

Chapter Thirteen

Shaun McMahon stood in the shadow of the trees and gazed up at the stars and the bright, full moon. He had parked his car well off the road, on the footpath next to the riverbank, and the only sounds he could detect along this deserted country lane were the trees rustling in the light breeze, the water gushing over the shallow edges of the river, and the occasional car in the distance.

Snorting impatiently, once every half minute or so, he looked at his watch, and once he hissed: "Come on you bastards!" He attempted to squint further up the lane as if waiting for somebody, then with another cross snort gazed up at the moon again.

Shaun McMahon was, and had always been, a victim of circumstance. Now, thirty-three years old, having once owned a lovely house near the Broads which was a reward for many years' hard work setting up his own window business, and having once been married to the woman of his dreams, he was now virtually back to where he had been when he left school. He had nothing.

At school he had not been successful. For some reason at that time he had not been able to get on with other pupils. He had learnt to fight well, but he had to because he was frequently being picked on. He wasn't small or weak, but there had still been something about him that the other boys hated. One time, a boy who had been bullying him had been asked why he wanted to bully Shaun, and the bully had replied that he could not answer this problem himself. He and his mates just hated McMahon.

McMahon had, however, got on quite well with some of the girls, particularly the school's favourite, a pretty, dark-haired girl called Maria Sweeney. By the age of thirteen she had already developed very womanly curves. She certainly had not been in love with McMahon, but she had been a very sensible, caring girl, often feeling sorry for him. She had even taken care of his wounds for him on more than a couple of occasions, gently washing and soothing his mouth and nose after he had been beaten up. He once thought that it had been worth the pain, just to experience the warmth and comfort from her afterwards.

He could have handled these problems, except that some of the teachers did not seem to like him either. He actually got picked on by certain members of staff, especially games teachers who appeared to be driving him harder than most of the other boys. And it was this, when he was fifteen, that eventually led to him being expelled from the school.

One day, a chemistry teacher who was standing in for the games tutor on sick leave, took McMahon's group for rugby. This teacher, a Mr Walters, was standing on the touchline hurling verbal abuse at some of the boys who, he felt, weren't working hard enough, but especially at McMahon. McMahon tried to take no notice. He got the ball and started running but was immediately brought down by Johnson, the school bully who then deliberately trod on his arm. McMahon got up fiercely and was about to take vengeance on the bully, when Walters yelled out.

"Sweeney can take care of it, McMahon. Tread on his bollocks next time, Johnson, I'm sure he'll appreciate that."

He had difficulty, afterwards, in remembering exactly how it happened, and it had seemed like a lifetime while the other boys stood in a circle around Mr Walters, waiting for the ambulance, grimacing down at his smashed face. All he remembered were Walters' words, briskly walking towards the chemistry master feeling all the anger which had been building up inside him for so long, followed by a sort of mental explosion. Then more teachers, ambulance men, and even the other boys began to move away while eyeing him suspiciously, talking to each other almost excitedly asking questions.

"How many times did McMahon hit him?"

"Don't know. Just ran into him like a steam train."

"Hundreds of times. We had to drag him off."

McMahon felt dizzy when he saw a police car turn up. He looked at his hands. They were covered in blood. For some reason he looked down at his rugby boots. They were also splattered with crimson ooze.

He was forced into therapy after that. The sessions were all about temper, how to control it, and how to cope with life's everyday little snags without wanting to punch somebody's face in. He knew, and his parents knew, that this was all wrong. He did not need this and had been treated totally unreasonably. However, he put up with it, realising that if he proved to the psychiatric nurses that he was okay, they would eventually leave him alone, pleased with themselves that it was they who had cured him.

This worked, and by the time he was seventeen, even with the blot of expulsion on his copy book, he'd managed to talk his way into a job as a door-to-door window salesman. And he began to do very well. He easily met the targets laid down for him by the company in his first six months, and a year later he was made regional manager.

On a social level, he began to enjoy life, and soon discovered that sales people enjoy an excellent social calendar. He began getting on with men, as well as women, and occasionally pondered over his old school days and wondered if the other boys would have liked him any better if he had been given a chance to get on with them. But after another year or two of good selling, making good money and buying his first house at the age of nineteen, memories of school soon faded away completely. It was one evening at a sales party, however, that he was given a reminder of one of the more pleasant sides of his school life.

He was at the bar buying a drink for himself and a middle-aged colleague, when he discovered that there, standing next to him, was an enchanting young lady with short, dark hair. He recognised her instantly as Maria Sweeney.

At nineteen, she had developed into a striking-looking, elegant young woman, and her low-cut, long evening gown showed her slim figure off to perfection. As he watched her, he thought that she seemed to be deep in a sort of trance, and when he softly said her name, she looked round, their eyes met, and her words were: "Oh, what a coincidence. I was just thinking about you." They came together with arms outstretched, and for a long moment they held onto each other. Then he moved back to look into her hazel eyes, and she held his face between her soft little hands and looked at him caringly, just the way she had done nearly six years before, after he'd received a bloody nose in a scrap.

It transpired that, the previous day, she had been for an interview for the vacancy of sales co-ordinator, and had been contacted by telephone that morning, offered the job which she had accepted, and then she had been invited to this sales do, where she could comfortably be introduced to many of her future colleagues from the various regions.

They talked of their old school days. She had not been around at the time of the Walters incident, but she had heard many different versions of the story. He told her the truth of what had happened, only leaving out the precise content of what Walters had said.

"It was about me, wasn't it?" she said seriously. "He said something insulting about me."

He put his arms round her again and held her close.

"You were my only real friend," he told her quietly.

"And you went to protect me," she whispered in his ear.

After the Walters incident, she had wanted to go and visit the McMahons to find out exactly what had happened, but her parents forbade her to go to him. They considered that any further association between McMahon and their daughter would be terribly ignominious to their family so they threatened her with all sorts of punishments if she disobeyed.

But the really important thing, as far as they were both concerned now, was that they had met again, and these were indeed excellent circumstances for a reunion. They continued to chat happily together for the remainder of that evening. They mixed with others for a little while, as she was supposed to be introduced to the most prominent personnel in the company, but they ended the evening together in a comfortable seat in the corner somewhere, and they held hands while they talked.

All too quickly, the evening was over. McMahon walked her to her car, and before she drove off, he told her he wished to see her again.

"You'll be seeing lots of me now," she laughed. "We're colleagues, remember?"

"You know what I mean," he smiled.

His reward was a huge, moist, smothering kiss which made blood rush around his whole body. All at once he started to feel unsteady on his feet and his knees felt like they were going to give way. She got into her car, gave him a cute little wave and a cheeky grin, blew him another kiss and drove off.

When he got home that night, he knew that he loved her. He wanted to be with her so much, it made him feel like crying. Crying with happiness that he could be in love with such a wonderful girl, but sadness and frustration that he wasn't actually with her, there, right that minute. This made him feel lonely but, paradoxically, energy welled up inside him which was his body's natural reaction in readiness to making love to her. He tried to sleep, but couldn't. Every time he closed his eyes, all he could see was her. Her face, her body, her smile, and the smallest details like all the feminine little gestures she made with her hands as she talked. And in his head he could still hear the soft tone of her voice and her laugh as he told her stories of his first few demonstrations out in the field as a salesman. He tried to think of other things to get rid of her from his mind so that he could sleep. He had a very important visit the next day which could lead to a contract with a new company putting new windows into their premises, a big office block, a deal which could be worth hundreds of thousands of pounds to his company.

It was no good. He still could not get that lovely young woman out of his head, and in the end he had to surrender to an extremely strong urge to hold his penis. He needed relief, so he took it. After masturbating, the warmth of his climax washed over him and, at last, he started to become more somnolent. Very soon after that, he fell into a comfortable sleep.

He won that big order, other orders kept pouring in, Maria Sweeney also did well in her job, getting on with all the company's important representatives, and within the year, McMahon and his childhood sweetheart were married. About the same time, McMahon thought of starting his own business, and began talks with financial people he knew who could help get him started.

When this idea eventually got off the ground, McMahon thought he had made a terrible mistake as orders came in slowly, but he took on a team of excellent sales and marketing people, and the orders soon began to pour in. Things could not have been better, and the newly-wed young couple were soon thinking about buying a bigger house in the most desirable area they could afford. They eventually bought a six bedroom cottage on the Broads, and for the icing on the cake, one night McMahon got home from an important sales meeting to find that Maria had prepared a very special meal. That evening, over the candlelit dinner, Maria let him have the news. She was pregnant. McMahon fairly leaped across the table, and hugged her so tightly she cried out, partly in excitement, and partly in pain. In about eight months he was going to be a dad - a complete success.

Then came the night of a terrible thunderstorm. Maria had decided that she would carry on working throughout her pregnancy, just as long as she could, and was working late at the office. McMahon was away for the day with two new prospective business partners, checking out some possible new premises with a view to expanding the company in the future. The storm started late in the afternoon and, with a hundred mile journey ahead of him, McMahon decided to quit from the new site earlier than planned, guessing that he should be home by about seven.

He wanted to let Maria know he was on his way home so, once he was on the motorway, at just before five, he phoned her works number from his car telephone, but was informed by her receptionist that she had just left. He smiled and sang to himself, despite the horrible weather, deciding to give her twenty minutes or so before trying again on their home number as she did not have a telephone in her car.

At twenty past five he tried the number, but no answer. At half past, and at twenty-five to six, he tried again but still no answer. The storm seemed to be getting worse, the rain fell in torrents and the traffic on the motorway was crawling. He switched on the car radio.

The news - an accident - involving two cars - a head-on collision. The descriptions of the cars were read out. One of them a light blue Toyota MR2, (the same model Maria drove) and one occupant, a young woman critically injured.

McMahon was stunned. It couldn't be Maria. It was just a terrible coincidence. He felt sorry for the poor girl, whoever she was, but it simply could not be his darling Maria with their unborn child. He stepped on the accelerator risking an accident himself. He would find out just to make sure. He could drive a bit faster if he was very careful, and possibly be home within the hour, by which time Maria would be home safe and well. As he drove faster, he tried his home number again. Still no reply.

Then the telephone bleeped making him react with such a violent start that he very nearly ploughed his car right up the backside of a huge lorry.

"Hello," he barked into the handset.

"Shaun McMahon?" came a sharp voice.

"Yes. Who's this?"

"Olney North Wing Hospital, Mr McMahon. Please could you get here as soon as you can. Your wife has been in an accident."

McMahon felt icy cold. This could not be happening. It had to be some rotten dream.

"On my way. Give me three quarters of an hour. How bad is she?"

"We'll discuss the full extent of the injuries when you get here, but please get here as soon as you can. She needs an operation, and we need signed permission to carry it out."

"But what..."

"Please be quick, Mr McMahon."

The line went dead.

McMahon was stunned. What operation could she possibly need which required a signed permission? It had to be the baby. She had lost the baby, it had to be. Or it was injured, or nearly dead or something, and they needed permission to abort it in order to save her. But it was no use speculating. He would just concentrate on driving through the storm as fast as possible, then he would learn what all this was about.

He arrived at the North Wing Hospital at 6.35 p.m., and was quickly and quietly ushered into a little waiting room. He was soon met by the doctor who came into the room, shut the door and sat down next to him.

"Hit me with it," McMahon said. "It's the baby isn't it?"

"We do understand that Mrs McMahon was pregnant," the doctor said gently.

"I knew it. That's it, but she's going to be fine?"

"I'm afraid that's not the problem," the doctor looked at him. "We're going to need your permission to..."

"What permission do you need? Surely you just do what's needed so she'll be okay."

"I'm afraid her legs have been totally crushed," the doctor explained. "I understand that the other car was on the wrong side of the road and the vehicles collided."

"What?" McMahon was shaking nervously. "She's broken her legs, do you mean?"

"I'm afraid we're going to have to amputate."

"No!" McMahon leaped to his feet. "Don't do that - she won't thank me for that. How would you feel? I mean I know if that was me I'd rather die than have bits lopped off me."

"In order to save her life," the doctor persisted. "If you love her you'll give us the chance to give her the chance, and we know from experience that people who are actually faced with this sort of choice do still want to live. Please?"

"But not both legs." McMahon was sobbing. He could not believe this was really happening.

"It's possible we may be able to save the right leg at the knee," the doctor continued.

"Let me see her," McMahon whispered.

"Of course."

But as it turned out, McMahon never had to make that decision.

He was led into the secluded ward where his wife was lying. He went in and sat next to her. He held her hand and looked at her face which seemed sort of rubescent, but showed no pain, or awareness. He realised that she was heavily sedated, but then she seemed to sense that he was there and her eyes fluttered and opened. He looked at her face, still beautiful and, once again, remembered how she had looked after him and comforted him after he had been beaten up at school.

He bent over her and held her head in his arms. They kissed for a few seconds.

"I love you," he whispered.

She gazed up at him.

"I love you, too," she murmured.

Then she let out a huge sigh, closed her eyes, and a few seconds later he realised that she was dead.

Again, Shaun McMahon peered up the dark country lane, still apparently expecting company.

"Come on, you bastards," he whispered.

Since his wife had died nearly twelve years ago, his life had gone completely downhill. All the money that he had amassed in his company had been spent on drink and drugs and paying fines. He had resorted to a life of crime to pay his way, but now he regretted wasting all that money. This evening's 'job' would be a nice big pay off, the idea of which would get him on his feet again. He still could not get over losing his beloved Maria, so cruelly taken from him, but he still knew that his life had to go on, and if he could get ahead of the game just once more then, this time, he would stay ahead. And so he, and three of his mates, had planned the great jewellery robbery. He had 'obtained' the second get-away vehicle, and now he was waiting for the three other guys to turn up with the first car but, so far, they were nearly fifteen minutes late.

"You bastards," he hissed again. "You'll cock up the whole plan."

Just then, something moved and caught his attention. In the moonlight, on the other side of the road near the shadows, he thought he saw something hop, or, he thought, it could have been a trick of the light with the tree moving slightly in the breeze. Then he heard a croak, followed by a weird, high-pitched squeal. Then he saw something moving, and definitely hopping. At first he thought it was a frog, but then realised it was too big and fat to be just an ordinary frog. He sauntered over to it, crouched down to take a closer look, and was fascinated by the creature which did seem to be a frog but, incredibly, had the unmistakable head and snout of a rat. And then the strangest thing occurred. It suddenly turned round, cocked its hind quarters up in the air, and spurted a jet of urine which caught McMahon full in the face. He fell over backwards, then sat up wiping his face on the sleeve of his coat. With an acrid taste in his mouth, he felt disgusted and began to spit in an attempt to remove the ghastly taste, but when he looked round again, the horrible creature had vanished. He spat on the ground a few more times, and the rotten taste did go away.

Then he saw a gleam of car headlights in the distance. The car was soon upon him. It stopped, and one of the three occupants got out. McMahon stood up and walked towards the car.

"You're late!" he shouted. "Is this the best you could do?"

He began to look around the old Vauxhall Astra.

"It's good enough," said the guy sitting behind the steering wheel - his mate, Wayne Dyson.

"What's our second car?" came a voice from the back seat of the car, a young fat lad called Nick King.

"A Celica," McMahon told them. "It's bloody fast."

"And what were you doing scrabbling around on your hands and knees?" asked Vic Besch, the other man who wore glasses with lenses like the bottoms of milk bottles.

"Oh, nothing," replied McMahon. "Come on, let's get going. We'll be late."

They left towards the town in the Astra, leaving the Celica half hidden on the path by the riverbank.

Chapter Fourteen

J.W. Howard glanced at the golden, star-shaped clock on the wall of his jewellery shop, and with the time at just after eight, decided to close. It had been a long day, but working a twelve-hour day once a week, which coincided with the nearby precinct and their working hours, was excellent for business. He locked the door and methodically began his locking up procedure.

First, the rings, watches, and all other displays in the windows were covered up in their trays with the alarm switches turned on. Then the glass cases inside the shop, and those at the front counter were locked, and the main alarm switch inside the shop was set. A little, yellow light began to flash slowly and this indicated that he now had forty seconds to leave the shop through the back entrance, and secure it behind him. On entering the shop again, of course, he had to remember that he had half that time to open the little door behind the counter and to push that main switch back again, otherwise the alarm would go off. In his twenty-eight years as manager of this shop, he had only ever forgotten that procedure once. The police had been there very quickly and, slightly embarrassed, he had the kettle on to make the boys in blue a nice cup of tea which he offered to them with his sincere apologies. They were very good humoured and had told him that at least his alarm system had now been properly tested.

He remembered the episode with a satisfied grin on his face. Good old J.W. He had gone home to his wife (God rest her soul) full of the story. He used to enjoy returning to his dear wife, Shirley, telling her all the news of his day, about the customers he had made friends with, what he had sold and how much money he had made from the business which they had started jointly. After she had got sick, though, he had run it on his own. When the doctors had diagnosed cancer he had nearly given up, but before she died she had made him promise, as her last wish, to continue with the shop.

He believed, honoured and valued everything she had ever said, and now the one thing that kept him going was the unshakeable belief that, one day, he would see her again. How could he not believe after the way they had met in the first place?

Whilst still a young man he had gone through bouts of depression. So bad were some of these that he decided to visit a fortune teller. First, for him, came the proof. He was told that between two certain dates (over a period of a week) he would suffer an accident which would stop him working for a couple of months. He had thought about this and had decided that the only form of accident he could imagine having would be a road accident, so he first decided that during this period he would refrain from using his car. Then, better still, he thought that he would not go out at all. He booked a week's holiday and stayed in his house the whole time. Then, on the Friday morning, a piece of stair carpet came away and tripped him. He fell down the whole flight of stairs and broke both his arms.

A couple of months later, as a firm believer in the fortune teller, he paid her another visit. This time he was told that at a certain place, at a certain time, he would meet the woman he would eventually marry. He was advised that, again there would follow a two-month period, during which he should plan wisely and very carefully, and to get properly organised.

At that place, and at that time, he was coming out of a lift and walked straight into the most lovely looking woman who was carrying a box of cream buns. The buns dropped out of the box and were squashed on the floor. J.W. and the lady both went down on their knees trying to sort out the mess. Then they looked up into each other's eyes at precisely the same moment.

"I would definitely like to get to know you," J. W. told her.

"Oh, really," she had replied. "Why?"

"Because we're going to get married," J. W. said.

And they were married. Precisely two months later.

With seconds to spare, J. W. gave the shop one final look round before switching off the lights and, closing the back door behind him, he then turned the key in the lock with a decisive click.

He nearly jumped clear of the pathway when suddenly, inexplicably, the alarm began to go off.

"Damn!" he muttered crossly to himself. "Must have done something wrong."

He turned the key back again, pushed the door open, switched the lights back on then raced into the shop. He immediately reached for the little door behind the counter and looked inside at the switch. As far as he could see, the switch was okay, except, of course, that now the red light was glowing.

Then he saw them. Four masked figures standing inside the broken doorway. One darkly-dressed man pointed a sawn-off shotgun right at his chest. The front door had been levered open, but he had not heard a sound from the back alley. J.W.'s mind began to race, inventing all manner of conclusions. Had they realised that he was still there? Was that part of their plan? Were they going to kill him?

Trembling, he put his hands in the air. Three of the men began smashing open glass cases with their heavy boots, filling bags with rings, brooches, bracelets, necklaces and valuable watches. The fourth man, the one with the gun, approached him.

"Ring the police," he ordered. "Tell them it's a false alarm."

"That won't do any good," J. W. stuttered. Then he immediately regretted saying this. Why should he give these thugs any helpful advice?

"Wadya mean?" growled the masked man, angrily pressing the shotgun into J. W.'s chin.

"It's the system," said J. W., petrified. "Don't you know? If an alarm goes, the police attend always, even if they know it's a false alarm before they arrive."

J. W. gritted his teeth, certain that he was about to be killed, but after an agitated pause, the masked man gestured over to the till.

"Open it, or you're dead."

J. W. inwardly scolded himself. There *had* been something he had forgotten. The day's takings should have been put in the safe. Fortunately, someone from the bank had already collected the morning's takings. He had a special arrangement as he was on his own. Now, some of the till's contents were cheques, and people had various methods of paying, but there was still around three hundred pounds cash in there. He opened it, then was immediately shoved out of the way, and brutally thumped on the back with the butt of the shotgun. He fell forward, coughing.

As the man grabbed the notes from the till, they all stood in silence. Then they heard the distinct note of approaching sirens.

"It's the filth!" yelled one of the men. "Let's go!"

At that moment, again, J. W. really thought that he was going to die. He saw the man with the gun suddenly brace himself and hold the weapon at chest height pointing it in his direction. As J. W. sat up behind the counter he saw the man's finger tighten its grip on the trigger.

"Shirley, help me," he whispered.

To his amazement the man suddenly spun round, and there was a deafening roar as the gun went off. Two of the other men flew backwards through the front window. J. W. crouched behind the counter with his hands over his face in an attempt to shield himself from the shower of glass and blood.

Then he heard the other man's voice.

"No, Shaun, what are you doing? Have you gone mad, or are you..."

There was a scream, then another loud explosion, followed by a sickening crash as the man's body landed across one of the glass cases.

The masked gunman then began rushing around the shop picking up the bags of jewellery. Confused and scared, J. W. stood up. He felt like vomiting at the sight that met him. A bloody carcass with it's head virtually blown right off, lying across the sea of glass fragments, and two dead men with gaping chest wounds lying outside on the pavement.

The masked man held the gun towards J. W.

"Take it," he said.

"What?" J. W. stuttered.

"Fucking well take the gun, old man!"

J. W. took the empty shotgun, then the masked man left through the back entrance.

Shaun McMahon took off his stocking-mask and stuffed it into his coat pocket. Such was his present mental state that he did not feel guilty any more just because the stocking used to belong to Maria. He had kept lots of her things since she had died including many of her clothes. He made his way across the street from the back entrance and up the road a little to where the Astra was parked. He looked back. There were quite a few people hanging around, but he had made the walk from the alley in such a cool manner that no one had taken any notice of him. The police would find enough to get their teeth into when they arrived at the shop, but when the old guy began to talk, they'd obviously be asking people nearby if they had seen anything. If anyone was bright enough to say that they had seen a guy with some bags getting into an old Astra, by that time he would be in the Celica and halfway across the country.

He drove away from the town, then towards the village where the second car would be still waiting. It was starting to rain a little now, and when he finally arrived, parking the Astra next to the Celica, he swore loudly when he noticed that he had inadvertently left the other vehicle's sunroof open slightly. Hoping that the seats had not got wet, he transferred the loot into the Celica's boot. He then went back to the Astra, reached in, released the handbrake, and watched as it slowly rolled into the river. He got into the other car, but then began to heave and choke. There was a really bitter smell coming from somewhere. It was so strong, he could taste something in the air, and he knew he had tasted that taste before, and very recently. Then, despite the rain which was now getting heavier, he opened all the windows fully and began to drive. The wind blowing through the car seemed to ease the horrible stench somewhat, but he decided that he might now need yet another car. He drove to the next town and looked around for a suitably quiet place to park. Eventually, he parked behind an old cinema, then climbed out of the car. It was a secluded spot so, for the time being, he decided to leave his evening's takings in the boot, and made sure the car was securely locked and all the windows were closed. After all, he did not want some bastard coming along and nicking it. Nothing was safe these days. 'You had to be very careful,' he told himself.

It was then that he heard the disco music. 'Great,' he thought. 'Ages since I've been to a night club. Might get a few beers in, too.' He checked his trouser pockets for cash, not wishing to break into the money from the jewellers already and, deciding that he had sufficient for a couple of hours, headed down the road following the sound of the music.

Chapter Fifteen

"I tell you, she's a totally different person," Celia Davey insisted as she spoke to her friends who had just arrived at the disco. "I just could not believe it."

"Get out of town," jeered one of them, a tall, lanky lad named John Balodis. "I wouldn't go out with a boring old bird like that."

"Yeah," agreed another, a fair-looking youth named Steve Beasley. "I prefer something with a bit more oomph." He raised his fist in the air and smacked himself on the forearm.

The others laughed. In all there were about eight of them, not counting Celia's boyfriend, Roger Barker, who had just excused himself for a minute. Apart from Celia, he was the only one who had seen the new-look Norma, and Celia was beginning to get suspicious concerning his whereabouts.

"Like I said," she continued, quickly glancing around her, "she came over to my place really dolled up, I mean apart from her clothes she looked great. All made up, her hair was nicely done, and I had to admit she looked fabulous."

"So why the change?" asked one of the other girls, a pretty red-head named Rita Kelly.

"That's what I asked, but she claims her image was all a front to fool us."

"Cobblers!" Balodis took a swig of beer and coughed noisily.

"Look," said Celia, "when you see her you'll have to admit that she does look absolutely marvellous. Anyway, like I said, she just needed a dress, so I gave her one of my mini skirts, you know, Rita, the one that looks like a long string vest, fishnet stockings and lacy undies. Honestly, she had to wear something underneath because the dress on its own is completely see-through, but that's the other thing…"

"What?" came an excited chorus.

"She seems to have changed so totally, I actually got the impression that she wanted to come out with a see-through dress with nothing on underneath."

"So where is this luscious thing now?" asked Beasley.

"Well actually, before you lot showed, I just..."

Everyone looked round in amazement, as Norma Richmond suddenly appeared at the table, followed closely by Roger Barker. The lads just sat there and gazed with their mouths hanging open. Balodis, taking another gulp of beer, stopped in mid-gulp then began to choke horribly until Rita got up and smacked him hard on the back. He coughed and spluttered.

"Sorry I was so long," said Norma. "We got talking at the bar and time just ran away with us."

Celia gave Roger a glare as he moved round the table to take his seat next to her. The other lads tried to guess where Norma was going to sit, and began to shuffle round hoping for the best view of those sensational legs. The mini skirt and fishnets really did suit her. In fact, Beasley considered that they looked better than they had done on Celia, and that was saying something. And the way she was made up. Everybody gazed at her for a while, but they noticed that her basic looks were not all that had changed. They soon discovered that her manner also was totally different. As they gazed at her, rather than shying away from their attention like the Norma of old, she stared back and, to the boys, she gave a sort of knowing, appreciative look as if she was asking them individually if they wanted her now on the table, or later somewhere in private.

"So." It was Beasley who broke the silence. "I hear you've been holding out on us."

"Yeah." A new, confident, seductive voice. "But it all got a little boring as you're all so easy to fool."

"Well, you certainly..."

"Let's dance," Norma abruptly got up as if she had just seen someone she wanted to meet.

"Why, sure." Balodis held his arm out to her as she pushed past, but she just flounced off with her nose in the air. As the disco party got under way with loud throbbing music, droves of obstreperous guys and girls surged out onto the dance floor.

Shaun McMahon tottered drunkenly towards the bar as the loud rock music began to play. He'd only had a couple of quick beers so far, but he already had a throbbing headache coming on which he attributed to the loud music. He spun around irritably as the sleeve of his jacket was grabbed.

"Watch it," he hissed, "you f..."

But there standing at his side was a gargantuan bouncer, six foot six of a mixture of fat and muscle and sporting a ridiculously small moustache.

"Excuse me please, Sir," the enormous individual said in a sarcastically polite voice. "I don't believe that you are a member here."

"A member?" McMahon was confused. The weird, muzzy headache he had coming on was making him feel dizzy. He was hot and he just wanted a drink.

"Sure," said the bouncer. "A member of the club."

"Oh, yeah, I joined recently." He was having to shout now as the music got suddenly louder and more people surged towards the dance floor.

"You joined recently, so who do you know here?"

McMahon looked around him.

"Well, I, er... my name is Shaun, and I..."

"Listen, Shauny baby, I know you're not a member, so save yourself a lot of pain by just leaving."

"Look," said McMahon, "I am a member, but all I want to do this evening is have a couple of quick drinks."

The bouncer let go of McMahon's arm.

"Sorry." He jerked his thumb over his shoulder towards the door. "Out, Shaun! Then you and I will part the best of pals."

McMahon failed to notice an extremely pretty girl in a short, see-through dress who had suddenly appeared at his side, and was looking on and listening to this exchange with a mixture of interest and curiosity, but it was his next remark which she found most intriguing

"Listen, pal," McMahon was still having to shout over the music, "you let me stay and I'll make it worth your while."

The girl noticed that the bouncer's eyebrows did rise briefly, but this was probably down to surprise, as he then became very nasty. He grabbed McMahon's arm again, then viciously twisted it round.

"I don't take bribes, not that a little shit like you could offer me anything..."

"You're wrong," McMahon grunted in pain, thinking his arm would break. "I've got thousands."

The girl in the mini dress acted quickly.

"Ah, Shaun," she yelled suddenly. "Late as usual. What's all this then?"

The bouncer gazed at her in surprise and eased his grip on McMahon's arm. McMahon also looked at her with surprise - and relief.

"You know this individual, Miss?" said the bouncer.

"Yes, he's my boyfriend," she grinned cheekily. "Always late, he joined the club recently, but if the silly thing's forgotten his card I'll vouch for him."

"Okay," said the bouncer in a slightly more cheerful voice. "Just so long as I've got a voucher."

Then looking at McMahon he said: "Next time might I suggest a smarter jacket and tie."

The music was beginning to die down as the bouncer made his way back towards the door. McMahon feasted his eyes on his attractive rescuer.

"I'm off for a drink," he said. "Want one?"

The girl nodded and smiled, then followed him towards the bar. He bought himself a beer, and she asked for a Bacardi.

"So," McMahon grinned after a long swig of beer. "You know my name, but..."

"My name's Norma." She sat cross-legged on a stool giving him a good view. "And what I want this evening is a bloody good time."

"I could give you that." He eyed her up and down. She was quite gorgeous, and he particularly admired her legs. He raised his eyebrows and his beer glass at these, as he liked fishnet stockings, and he liked the bare, cheeky bits at the top which were just in view, but she could have hardly been seventeen or eighteen. At least not under age. He grinned to himself.

She was looking into his face all the time and enjoying the way he had looked admiringly at her legs and everywhere else, and she had noticed his lecherous grin.

"Are we out for the same thing?"

"Of course."

He took another long gulp of beer, then almost choked. He was getting a hard on.

Then she suddenly leaned forward, put her hand on the inside of his upper thigh where it increased the pressure on his growing tool, and put her face very close to his.

"I heard you telling that bouncer that you could make it worth his while if he let you stay."

"Oh, yes, well, that was..."

"And that you had got... thousands. Thousands of what, exactly?"

'Christ,' thought McMahon. 'Maybe she was older than she looked and was a policewoman, or something.' But then he began to laugh. For some stupid reason he just didn't care anymore. This headache was beginning to muddle his thinking, he mused. Maybe, if he told her about what he had done and she did turn out to be a policewoman, it would be all right. He would be arrested, he would go to prison, but eventually he would get released and start afresh and get a good honest job like he'd had before. Maria would be looking down at him now from Heaven. It was the first time he had thought of that. She would be disappointed - disgusted. He didn't want her to feel that way. And another concern was even if he did get away with this crime in this present life, one day he might meet Maria again, and she would have to sit and watch as they adjudicated his doings.

"Look Norma," he suddenly blurted out. "I'm a criminal, I wasn't always one, I used to have my own company but now I'm in the gutter. I've just robbed a jewellers and the boot of my car is crammed full with watches, expensive jewellery and cash. In short, you don't want to know me."

Norma tilted her head back and drained her glass, then she looked at him seriously.

"You're under arrest," she said.

"Brilliant! I knew it."

Norma roared with laughter.

"I was only joking," she croaked.

"What? Oh, Christ."

"Were you being serious?"

"Yes, and really you don't want to know me?"

"You're wrong?" Norma put her arm round him and rested her hand on his bottom. "Let's get the hell out of here. I'll help you sort out all your problems, and you can show me the loot in your boot."

"Okay," McMahon laughed, feeling a bit better now. "Wait here. I'm just going for a piss."

He went back to the door and towards the toilets, passing the bouncer on his way. In the men's room he walked past a mirror and became aware that the bouncer was following him. He spun round.

"Hi," he said a little apprehensively.

"Listen mate," said the bouncer, "I guess you must have something to have a bird like that?"

"So?" McMahon was suspicious of this fat old boy.

The bouncer grinned and continued slowly towards him. He began rubbing his knuckles.

"So, my little friend, you said you would make it worth my while if I let you stay."

"But I'm a member."

Suddenly, the bouncer grabbed him by the neck and pinned him to the wall.

"You're no more a member than my great aunt. Now, you said you had thousands."

"Yes," McMahon croaked. "Look, I've got an idea, maybe we could help each other."

The bouncer let him go.

"Okay, I'm listening, but this better be good!"

"That bird I'm with," McMahon grinned slyly, "I need to really impress her."

"Impress her?"

"Yes, you know, so that later I can... well, you know."

"You mean you haven't..."

"No, not yet."

The bouncer, for once, relaxed slightly, becoming almost amicable. "You're having me on."

"I need to impress her," McMahon continued, "with how brave I am. She's a bit like that. Likes to see a good fight."

The bouncer's eyes narrowed

"Maybe I had better..."

"No, no, no," McMahon said hastily. "You're not really her type."

The bouncer raised a clenched fist.

"Don't take the piss, boy."

"I'll give you..." McMahon paused, "three hundred quid to pick a fight with me outside in full view of my bird, then let me hit you a couple of times. After that you hit the pavement in a state of unconsciousness."

There was actually a laugh on the big bouncer's face.

"Five," he said.

"What?"

"Five. Five hundred quid, or I'm chucking you out the back entrance right now."

"Okay, okay." McMahon knew he could be in trouble as he only had three hundred quid cash, but maybe the big beefcake would accept an expensive watch.

"Just let me go for a piss, then I'll go and get my bird, and we're leaving."

"Right," said the bouncer, "But you double cross me, and it'll be you hitting the pavement."

When McMahon arrived back at the bar, Norma had gone. He quickly looked around, then he saw her chatting to some other lads. He went over to them, and as he did he heard one of them saying: "But, Norma, you can't just go off with this guy, you don't even know him."

"Hello, there," he called out.

"You took your time," said Norma. "Thought you'd got lost."

"Sorry about that. Ready?"

"Yes."

Without another word, Norma started for the door, and before McMahon followed, he glanced at one of the other lads who gave him a very aggressive stare in return.

Outside the sudden cold air hit McMahon like a tidal wave but he was sure that the dull throbbing inside his skull was beginning to subside.

Norma and McMahon began walking arm in arm, and as they chatted, he almost forgot about the next part of the plan. When it happened, everything seemed to occur so quickly he didn't even have time to think.

"You!"

A now familiar, gruff voice accompanied by a meat-hook of a hand on his shoulder. Norma was pushed to one side as the bouncer landed a heavy blow into McMahon's stomach. McMahon doubled up in pain and dropped to his knees. This was most certainly not in the script. Then Norma screamed and flung herself at the bouncer. He yelled in pain and surprise when he felt her long, painted fingernails dig deep grooves down his cheek. McMahon got to his feet but only to watch in disbelief as Norma continued to scratch, punch and kick their attacker before the bouncer managed to push her off. McMahon took one step forward, still ready to make this person earn some of his five hundred quid, when Norma unleashed the most awesome, fearful kick and, with pointed shoes, landed it squarely into the bouncer's scrotum. The wretched man screamed horribly as he dropped to his knees and fell sideways. Blood was oozing from wounds on his face made by Norma's long nails.

But still the event wasn't over. McMahon heard shouts of "Norma, wait!" coming from up the road. Looking round he recognised the lads Norma had been speaking to earlier.

Norma pointed at the grovelling bouncer on the floor.

"That bastard attacked us for no reason!"

McMahon could not help laughing when the four lads jumped on the temporarily crippled hardman and commenced giving him a kicking he would never forget. Soon he had a nose which resembled a squashed tomato.

But Norma seemed quite prepared to leave her friends to it.

"Come on," she tugged McMahon's arm. "Let's get out of it."

They ran together and he led the way to the alley where he had left the Celica.

"Here we are," he said opening the boot. He opened up one of the bags.

"Wow," she said as she feasted her eyes on all the jewellery.

"And this one's just for you," he told her, picking out a necklace with lots of different coloured gems. He put his arms round her and placed the necklace gently round her neck. "For looking after me, and protecting me against grievous bodily harm." He then laughed, remembering that it should have been him protecting her, and paying five hundred quid for the privilege. His thoughts were distracted when he heard the siren of a police car coming from up the road. "Better get going," he told her.

The smell in the car seemed to have completely vanished, so McMahon did not, for tonight, have to worry about getting another car. They drove towards the motorway which would take them further north.

As they hit the motorway Norma said: "Where exactly are you taking me?"

"We've got plenty of cash," McMahon told her, "so I guess we'll find a little hotel somewhere, then I'll have to dump the car sometime tomorrow 'cos it's hot."

"That's a shame." Norma leaned over towards him and placed her hand between his legs. "I like this car. I'd love to have sex in a car like this."

"Would you?"

He took an admiring glance at her.

"Sure," she purred, still with her hand pressed between his legs. "It would be kinda cosy."

McMahon coughed, looked at the speedometer and saw that he was cruising nicely at seventy. He laughed, and instinctively, with the pressure of her hand on his hardening prick, went to stretch out his legs. The affect of this was that his foot went to the floor on the accelerator.

The car began to pick up speed and, at eighty miles an hour, Norma began unzipping his flies.

He started to grunt and groan, then he looked at the speedo again. They were doing ninety-five and she had his rock hard penis in her hand.

McMahon laughed and grunted.

He was in the outside lane overtaking everything. Then at 100 mph he overtook a police car, looked in the rear-view mirror, and blasphemed under his breath when he saw it pull out after him with the blue cone on.

It was when they were doing 110 mph that Norma leaned right over and pulled him into her mouth. Instinctively he began to bounce up and down. Again he looked in the rear-view mirror and saw the police car gaining on them and flashing its lights.

It all happened at once. The early model 1600 GT Toyota Celica hit its flat-out, maximum speed of 115 mph. Bouncing in his seat, McMahon exploded in an uncontrolled wave of ecstasy. Unfortunately, they crossed a bridge at this precise moment, and McMahon's hands slipped off the steering wheel, throwing the car into a violent swerve. It ploughed through some temporary barriers, and its engine screeched as it became airborne. It then nose-dived into the ground below, blowing up on impact in a brilliant ball of flame.

Chapter Sixteen

Franklin Jackson had had little luck with the ladies lately. It was not as if he wasn't good looking - far from it. He was over six feet tall, very slim and dark, and he had kept himself fit. He was thirty-five, but he looked ten years younger, and played as central defender in his local football side who were currently top of the regional league, and although he was in defence he did occasionally get on the score sheet. He had, in the past, been quite a hit with the ladies, but for now at any rate, it seemed, his luck had dried up.

He did, however, have one little fetish - he loved his women fat. Roly-polys, with sexy fat hips to grab hold of, rolls of flesh around the arms, legs and tummy, but most of all he loved the ones with huge, soft breasts. Most fat women, he knew, had extra big bosoms because of the fat, and he knew from experience that most plump girls made very randy, passionate lovers. While the man was enjoying sinking into all that lovely, warm, soft flesh, they were in turn enjoying the feeling of smothering the groaning, moaning man with their bodies. It made them feel powerful, he concluded, and these were the women for whom Jackson had the very greatest desire.

He had once dated the best friend of his mate's girlfriend, an extremely plump young girl called Gwendoline, just to make up a foursome, then out of politeness had accepted her invitation to her flat at the end of the evening, and had gone in for a quick cup of coffee. She was very plump indeed, but had a reasonably pretty little face and had nice eyes. He had not had much out of her in the way of conversation all evening, though, so he thought she was just a little shy, and had also decided that she was probably somewhat inexperienced in friendships and relationships.

After a few minutes of general conversation he coughed politely as a prelude to saying goodnight, and wondered whether or not to give her a little goodnight kiss, but then at the last moment decided against the idea for fear that a girl who must be so callow would think she was about to be raped. He was then exceedingly surprised when she started to get undressed, began to undress him and, all of a sudden, was suggesting that they should go to bed. The sight of the rolls of flesh on her soft, freckly body, all at once began to excite him. He put his arms around her and attained the quickest erection he had ever experienced. She was lovely, so soft and warm. He simply could not get enough of her. They did go to bed and made love three times before falling asleep in each other's arms. Actually, after all that, he had wanted to make love again, but she decided that because they hardly knew each other, they should both be patient.

After that weekend, at work he saw his mate who came up to him and said: "Thanks for the other night, Frank. You won't have to endure another evening like that, I promise." His mate was very surprised to be told that Franklin and Gwendoline were going to see each other again, and amazed to learn that Gwendoline was "a real little goer".

But, alas, after some months, Gwendoline moved on, her job as marketing agent taking her away up north, and that was that. Apart from being disappointed at losing his plump bird, Franklin was left with a desire for more fatso females, and over the next year or two dated many such girls, and was quite satisfied to find that they all made excellent lovers.

Then he decided to settle down and get married to a fairly plumpish girl, but soon got bored with her when she got in with some fitness freaks and began to lose weight. He was always being told by his mates how much better she looked and how thrilled he must be with her, but the truth was that he was extremely bored with her. He no longer fancied her.

So, after a lot of consideration, and much deliberation, he placed a personal advert in his local newspaper, but mindful of the fact that no decent girl would give him a second glance once she learned of his marital status, at first he decided to put in the advert that he was single, but then he realised that this could cause problems if the girl subsequently wanted to telephone him at home. So what he did was explain about all his desires to his wife advising her of his dissatisfaction with her, and told her that he wanted to make love to plump girls, and that he would place a personal advertisement to attract such women.

His advert ran:

> *"35 year old male, tall, dark and handsome, separated, would like to meet females between 25 and 35, would prefer a woman with the 'fuller' figure for romantic nights in, and plenty of this, that and the other."*

This appeared in his local newspaper and attracted an absolutely huge response. He was overwhelmed with the number of replies - over fifty recorded messages in one week.

The following week he began to contact the girls, one by one, arranging to meet those he particularly liked the sound of. He appreciated a sexy voice, and lots of chubby girls, he knew, had sexy voices, but before he gave his own telephone number to any of them he warned them that, although he was separated, he was now actually still sharing his house with his current wife and so, therefore, there might be an occasion when she would answer the telephone. In the first instance this did not deter any of them. They were obviously all too anxious to get down to business, and grateful for this opportunity.

For the next four weeks, his opinion about fat girls being amorous and randy and sometimes quite kinky, was strengthened. The first girl he met was a very glamorous looking girl called Haidee. She was twenty-seven, and plump but she had an absolutely beautiful face, and lovely long, curly, brown hair. She had hazel eyes, luscious lips, and Franklin just stood there with his mouth hanging open when he first saw her. They arranged to meet in a pub. Earlier that day on the telephone, they had described themselves to each other, and said what they would be wearing so that they would recognise each other without any embarrassing messing about. She was wearing a mini skirt, which was nice because some fat girls think they should hide their legs, but she was obviously proud of her thighs which, although large, were still quite shapely.

They sat and chatted for a couple of hours, then when it was time to go, they had a little kiss goodnight but, at first, she did not seem to be sure about him coming back to her place, or even seeing him again. However, she had his telephone number, he had hers, and he hoped they would see each other again sometime soon.

Next he contacted a girl called Jeril, and the moment he saw her he somehow knew that they could minimise the nonsensical 'breaking the ice' period. She was also quite pretty, but wore no make-up, and, aged thirty-one, had a rosy fresh complexion. When they sat down in the pub together, she removed her velvet jacket, showing a low-cut, sleeveless dress which showed off her podgy chest, and bare plump arms. He went to hold her hand, and she held his hand in both of hers. She looked into his eyes. She had the lightest blue eyes he had ever seen. Even the touch of her soft, little hands was giving him an erection. After just half an hour, she made an excuse about the smoky atmosphere, and invited him back to her house.

First she wanted to take a shower, then called him up to wash her back, and inevitably he ended up in the shower with her. Her rolls of soft pink flesh dripped with loads of soapy, steaming water while she gently bathed his penis and balls in soapy bubbles. It proved too much for him, and his knees began to buckle as he climaxed into her hands. She squealed with delight as some of his warm semen shot over her tummy. She continued to wash the rest of him while he recovered. Then they got out of the shower, dried each other, and she told him to go down to the kitchen to make some coffee whilst she went to her bedroom to get something she needed. He was just about to put on his trousers, but she told him there was no need as there was no one else around. She told him it would be nice if he just walked around in the nude.

Totally starkers, he was standing in the kitchen waiting for the kettle to boil, when Jeril re-appeared. She was wearing a very tight, brief, black plastic bra, and plastic panties to match. These were so tight on her they made her flesh bulge, and he loved the way her thighs wobbled when she moved, from one side to the other, bending and leaning her body either way, shifting the weight from one leg to the other as she spoke.

"You like?"

He could feel a new erection developing and he came to her.

"You are gorgeous," he told her.

She laughed a sort of deep, wicked laugh as he put his arms around her. They kissed passionately, but suddenly she pushed him away.

"Are you into kinky games?" she asked huskily.

"Oh, yeah," was all he could think of saying.

"Come on."

She took him by the hand and led him into the lounge.

"Just let me do this," she told him quietly. "Just sit and enjoy. I won't hurt you."

She sat him in an armchair, then with a soft, red piece of cord began to tie his feet together. He protested slightly when she firmly pulled his arms behind his back and tied his hands together, but all the time he kept gazing at her podginess and, totally overcome by this, he gave in to her.

"Just let me know if I'm tying these too tightly," she told him. "I don't want to stop your circulation, but for maximum enjoyment, for you and me, you really must be unable to escape."

When she finished tying his hands, with a third piece of cord, she tied his body to the chair, so, totally naked, he really was her captive now. She then began to move around him so he could watch her wobbling fleshy body in front of him, but he couldn't move. Then she went to the CD player in the corner of the room and put some soft, seductive music on. He tried to free his hands, but realised, with a mixture of excitement and fright, that he couldn't budge.

In her tight, black, plastic bra and panties, she began to gyrate to the music in front of him, and the sight of her soft, pink wobbling flesh, coupled with the fact that he was bound to the chair, gave him a huge erection. Then she reached behind her television set and produced a Polaroid camera.

"Er, no, no," said Franklin. "I don't think so."

She started clicking away, taking pictures of him, naked, aroused, and tied to a chair, from lots of different angles. 'The fat witch was not just into bondage,' he thought with growing panic. She was into humiliation as well. He looked round nervously expecting her to produce a whip.

"Oh, I hope you don't mind," she chuckled softly as she continued to take pictures. "I just love doing this."

"I hope you're going to destroy those pictures," he told her crossly.

"Certainly not, they're for my collection."

By virtue of the fact that he had allowed her to tie him up in the first place, she had taken this as his acquiescence in the photo session. As countless pictures were placed across the carpet in varying degrees of development, Jeril replaced the film.

"Now stop getting cross and start smiling for these pictures."

"No," said Franklin. "Now cut me loose, you fat cow."

Jeril knelt down in front of him with her camera in one hand, and with the other hand she grabbed hold of Franklin's testicles. She squeezed just very slightly.

"Now are you going to look as though you're enjoying yourself?"

"Ow, yes," Franklin howled. "Please let go."

"Now you're losing your hard on." She stood up, furious. "That's no good."

With her free hand she began slapping him hard across the face.

Then there was a knock at Jeril's front door. At first Franklin believed that he had been rescued and heaved a sigh of relief.

"Thank fuck!" he breathed. "Now for fuck's sake, you demented bitch, untie me."

But to his disappointment, she did not untie him. To his surprise, she only paused for a moment, then smiled. And to his utter amazement, she went out to the hall without going to get dressed, and answered the door. He could hear another voice from the hall - a female voice, then the sound of the door closing. Then in came Jeril followed by another plumpish looking girl who had sort of Latin looks with short dark hair. And she was carrying a video camera. He had a strong suspicion now that things were about to get a lot worse.

"Oh, lovely," said the new girl, looking at Franklin.

"Please untie me now," he said.

The dark girl wasted no time. She focused her video camera and started filming while Jeril continued to gyrate around the room to the seductive music. Franklin continued to watch her but, as yet, to Jeril's disappointment, his erection was not returning. Then she knelt down in front of him and began to caress him gently, and then the sight, and the sound, and the feel of her made him begin to enjoy the situation a bit more, and he began to relax.

"Ah, that's better," she said softly as he stiffened in her hands. "Good boy, that's much better."

He leant forward and kissed her. She laughed softly and undid her bra and panties so that she was now totally naked. He could see the marks that the tight, plastic things had made in her flesh. Then, as the other girl was continuing to film, Jeril put her arms around him, sat on his lap, and allowed him to kiss the upper parts of her body. Then she turned round, sat on him so that she held his erect tool up between her own legs, and tried to look as if she had a penis and she was masturbating. The dark girl came in closer for a close up, and zoomed in on the genitalia.

Then Jeril got off him, moved round behind him, and began to untie him from the chair, although she kept his hands and feet tied. She moved in front of him again, then lay down and pulled him down on top of her.

"Give it to me," she grunted.

Franklin Jackson, despite having his hands tied together, and his feet bound together tightly, proceeded to have the most explosive sexual encounter that he had ever experienced. The dark girl continued to record the happy event with her video camera, then later Jeril made a copy of the tape using her own video machine, and gave the copy to Franklin as an insurance policy, promising private viewing only, and they all finished up in the shower together which rounded off a truly memorable occasion.

It was a week or so after his experience with Jeril. Franklin was at home doing some washing up, when the telephone rang. It was Haidee, the first girl he had met.

They agreed to meet at the same pub as before, sat and talked for about an hour, and this time she invited him back to her house. She made a cup of tea and sat down next to him on the sofa, but Franklin decided not to expect too much, as she did seem to be rather shy - certainly nothing like Jeril!

As she sat chatting about general things, like dental appointments and shopping, he took time just to look at her. Looks-wise, she certainly was better than Jeril. He remembered thinking how beautiful she was when they first met. Her long, curly brown hair, and hazel eyes set off a very pretty complexion but, unlike that demented nympho, she did wear some make-up. She was wearing a white, lacy blouse and, Franklin noticed, she had on the same tight, red mini skirt she had worn a week or so earlier. He thought she looked quite fabulous but, he was just smiling to himself thinking how unlikely it would be for her to suddenly came on strong like the previous one had done in her tight plastic underwear, when she said: "Do you fancy going to bed?"

At first, he thought that he had imagined it. She read his widening mouth, and silence, and stammering, as: "Yes, I'd very much like to, but I'm too shy, and too much of a gentleman to actually admit it."

"Come on."

She daintily held out her hand, took his, slowly stood up, then led him up the stairs and to the bedroom. She sat him on her bed and began to undress him. Then she undressed herself as he watched. Although she did indeed have a full figure, Franklin decided, she was still very shapely, had all the curves in the right places, and had beautifully shaped breasts. She was definitely of the ripe and voluptuous sort, and he wondered, after all, if she could be just a little on the salacious side. Anyway, he knew he wanted her, and he also realised that he could not resist her for much longer. When he stood up and put his arms around her, without thinking he held her as tightly as he could and squeezed her.

"Uh," she grunted, partly in pleasure and partly in pain. "It's ages since a man held me like that."

"Oh, sorry, my darling," he whispered, loosening his grip on her body ever so slightly. She was so soft and warm that, once again, he found himself with an instant hard-on.

"That's all right," she whispered, kissing his bare chest and licking his hairy nipples. "I know I'm beautiful. All the boyfriends I've ever had have always told me so."

"You *are* beautiful," he gasped, kissing her all over her neck and shoulders.

She laughed softly and whispered: "And you're not too bad yourself."

Their naked bodies leaned over together, and they fell onto her soft bed. First they cuddled, and squirmed and wriggled around together. Then Haidee pulled back the blankets, and they began to get in together.

"Nothing kinky," she said suddenly. "Just straight sex, okay?"

"I'm you're man," Franklin assured her with a sigh of relief. Although he had mainly enjoyed his encounter the other evening with Jeril and her friend, he did not feel in the mood to be videoed having kinky bondage sex with a nymphomaniac, or some other such nonsense.

It was then, however, that he detected a crinkley sort of quality to the inside of the bed, and discovered that the bottom sheet was made of plastic.

"Oh, plastic," he whispered more to himself than to Haidee. "How cosy."

"Oh, do you mind?" she snuggled up to him when she felt his hardness pressing into her. "It's just that I do tend to sweat a lot."

"No, of course it's okay."

She pulled the top covers up, and cosily wrapped herself and Franklin up together in them. Their kissing gradually became more urgent, and their bodies bounced and rolled comfortably around together. They made happy, contented, grunting noises.

Then she stopped moving, became silent and, momentarily, stopped breathing.

"Piss on me," she whispered, "please, just a little."

"What?" Franklin gasped.

He could not believe it. He was disgusted, but then he thought he must have misheard. She must have really said: "Is this all me," or something.

"Please?" she moaned. "Just a couple of drops, it turns me on so much."

He had actually heard of this phenomenon before. It was like an animal instinctively needing to mark its territory, and dogs and cats often attracted their mate's attention by means of smell, and this meant urinating a little. But he knew that if he urinated, he might not be able to maintain his erection, or he'd have to work like the clappers in order to obtain another erection.

"Do it," she moaned loudly. "Please get on with it."

It was hard work at first, but at last he managed a wee jet of urine through his hardened penis.

She instantly exploded like a woman possessed. She went completely berserk, and somehow gathered the strength of ten women. She jerked and pushed until he went over side. She slapped and clawed at him, then amazingly, she was on top and he was being pinned down with the most unbelievable, ferocious strength. Her hands were pinning his arms down on either side of his head, her long painted nails were digging into him, and she started growling, snapping and snarling like some angry, wild tigress ferociously biting his ears. In his mind's eye he suddenly caught a vision of the teenage girl in *The Exorcist* film and wondered if this woman was like her - possessed by a demon. He hoped that she would not puke a gushing torrent of yellow bile all over him.

Instead he felt warmth and moisture on his penis, balls, and lower abdomen. She was urinating on him. He'd never known a feeling like it. She must have had nearly a full bladder because it seemed to be going on and on. It was warm and comforting, and as the flow of warmth began to die down, so her body began to relax and he was able to move. His erection was strong again, and, while she still lay on top of him, panting and still exhausted from her premature orgasm, he managed to insert himself into her. It was the most relieved, comfortable, lazy sexual experience he'd ever had.

He did not, however, get to enjoy much laziness, for next she wanted to go downstairs again and, while still naked, run around together in her back garden. She simply wanted them to continue behaving like animals.

On stepping out the back door before her, he paused.
"The neighbours might see," he advised her
"It's late," she giggled.
"They might hear us, then they might..."
"It is quite dark, you know."
"It's a full moon." He had serious doubts. "Still light enough."
"It's more fun if someone sees us," she laughed breathlessly. "Now come on, scaredy cat."
Then he turned back one more time.
"It's raining."
She put her hands on her hips, put her head on one side and pulled an impatient face, and Franklin had to admit she looked gorgeous.

"You're hardly going to get your clothes wet," she said, then she pushed him sharply in the back, and together they were out, totally naked, in the middle of a summer night, but in the pouring rain.

They ran and played together, like a pair of children, running and laughing, sometimes holding hands as they ran in circles, but other times chasing each other.

Then, after a while, all of a sudden, quite breathless, she stopped. She stood still, parted her legs and bent over slightly with her hands on her hips. And she began to urinate again. Franklin was amazed that she had any piss left in her. While still doing this she looked at him with her rain-soaked hair plastered across her face, and roared with laughter when she saw his astonished, wide-eyed expression.

It was while she was crouching, doing something out of her rear passage, that he noticed some movement from the corner of the garden. There in the moonlight, he just caught sight of it. Curious, he went to have a closer look. At first he thought that it was a frog, but there was something strange about its size, its shape and the way it moved.

"Hey, whatya doing?" came an almost insane, excited cackle from Haidee.

By the time he had realised what was so unusual about this frog, he also saw that the garden was now swarming with seemingly thousands of them, and by the time he had correctly guessed that they could be dangerous, he was engulfed with them as they jumped onto his naked, wet body.

He fell over and threshed around on the slippery grass trying to slap them off, and screamed when they began to bite into him. The unbelievable agony of having his balls chewed off drowned out the sound of Haidee screaming..

With his genitals gone, pouring with blood and now in shock, he managed to get to his feet one last time. He was temporarily free of the hideous animals as they greedily fed upon the bloody scraps in the wet grass. He ran towards the garden shed, and would have made it if he had not slipped over again. That was his last chance gone as a swarm of frograts chased after him, leaped onto him, and commenced to suck the blood and chew off more pieces.

As the fat, naked girl carried on screaming through this terrible nightmare, she continued to pass her body's waste out onto the grass, now out of sheer fright. She was so petrified that she didn't even wonder why these foul-looking creatures continued to hop around her, and pass her by, without actually attacking her.

They continued to slurp and gnaw bits off the dying body of Franklin Jackson.

Chapter Seventeen

Alison Bunning sat in her car and cried. Every conceivable problem and piece of rotten luck had built up over a period of time, and had culminated in such a terrible feeling of hopelessness and despair, she could barely face up to life any longer. Everything at last seemed pointless. All she could do was to sit there in reminiscence of the previous ten years. She tried, as she had been advised, to remember the good times as well because there had been plenty of those, but her efforts were futile because the good times had, all too often, ended in something bad happening. Ultimately, an unbearable tragedy had occurred. There was no future, and no point in continuing. She had finally hit rock bottom.

She was a teacher, and a very good one, and at least she still had her job. That Monday morning she had parked her car in her usual place in the school car park, but then, looking towards the doors of the front entrance, through tear-filled, blurred eyes, she seriously contemplated not going in. She leant forward, held her face in her hands, and wept.

She used to be the headmistress of the school, but because of the stress, and after consultation with the authorities, it was amicably agreed that she should step down from the principal's position, but to be able to continue teaching the ten and eleven-year-olds — the top class in the primary school. The substantial drop in salary did not bother her unduly. She was from a rich family and, she was in her own right, quite a wealthy woman. She owned two large cottages (one of which she rented out), and she shared part of a farm where she kept her four horses.

She was indeed a very good teacher having taught all over the world. Her main subjects were languages. She had taught French whilst living in Germany, German in Italy, Italian in France, and had taught English as a foreign language to Asians. She had also taught geography in American schools, together with mathematics, science and history.

Whilst in Germany she had met a ship's captain and had fallen completely and hopelessly in love. At first he had appeared to be the kindest, gentlest, most generous man that Alison had ever met. It was ten years ago now - she was just twenty-nine years old, whereas he was forty-one but still very young-looking and extremely handsome. She was a very virtuous type of woman and had allowed only one previous boyfriend to make love to her, but the captain had made love to her on so many occasions before they were finally married that she had lost count. And then she started to take time off work so that she could sail on his ships, and his insatiable lust for her meant that he was in her berth the whole time.

Then, one evening, for no apparent reason, he became drunk, and abusive towards passengers whilst in charge of the vessel. He was inevitably reported by his second-in-command and was kicked off the ship — almost literally.

Alison was shocked at the time, but also somewhat confused at his attitude towards his career as he just didn't seem to care, but it transpired afterwards that he had two or three other businesses with other people running them in his absence. The businesses included short-distance shuttle fights, and a driving school. These, at first glance, seemed quite respectable. One evening, however, just over two years ago, while he was out for the evening somewhere, partly out of curiosity but partly out of boredom, she went through some of his papers which he kept in a box file, on a shelf in the study of their house. She found a letter from a bank which said that after much consideration they had decided against the proposed business transaction. Attached to this was a business plan which Alison understood because she had filled in one of them whilst still a college student. It showed the commencing balance in red. Her eyes widened at the figure. It represented a huge debt, but then under the first month's income was another huge figure. The balance under this, a moderate figure was written in black. Business had suddenly picked up, she concluded. Then, as she turned to the next page, a letter dropped out. She picked it up and instantly recognised the bank's letterhead. She read it.

It ran:

> Thank you for the cheque which is duly signed by yourself. Although this is a joint account, because of the large sum being withdrawn, and because your wife originally opened the account, we must have her signature on the back of the cheque. We therefore return this to you.

Alison continued to shuffle through the papers, then found another letter from the bank. This one was dated about a week after the first one. It ran:

> Thank you for the cheque signed by yourself and countersigned by your partner. I am happy to tell you that this transaction may now commence.

She went rigid, then felt hot and cold at the same time. She blew her cheeks out angrily, then picked the box file up and turned it upside down until everything dropped out. She spread everything out. There were other letters and loose pieces of paper. Then she saw a letter in her own handwriting. It was a letter which she remembered writing to him before they were married. It had her usual signature at the bottom. Then she saw them - a wad of papers fastened together with a paper clip, and on them was what looked like her signature, written and re-written many times. Some looked better than others, but generally as her eye followed the list downward, they got better and better. Then, thumbing her way directly to the bottom sheet she found the perfect copies of her signature. She was sweating now, and shaking. She could not believe it. He had forged her signature to obtain a huge some of money from a savings account which she herself had originally opened years before they had been married. The money in there had by no means represented all her savings, but there had been a substantial amount of money.

She looked back at the incoming figure on the first month of the business plan. Ninety thousand pounds. She left the study, leaving the contents of the box file on the table, and went to find her bank books and savings accounts books and statements. She found all her books and statements where she expected to find them, except the pass book for that one account from which her husband had drawn that large some of money.

By the following day, her husband had still not returned, so she telephoned the bank, quoted the account number and asked for a statement for that account. The confused man in the bank told her that the account was now closed, reminding her of the last withdrawal.

"You will send me a full statement anyway," she demanded. "I want every detail over the last three years."

When, two days later, she received the statement, her worst fears were realised. Over a period of three years, her husband, the man she had loved and trusted totally, had had over three hundred thousand pounds out of her. She felt like she wanted to die, not because of the huge financial loss, but because of the massive betrayal.

With no questions asked she filed for divorce. To add insult to injury, though, she had to leave the house, a house that she had bought before they had been married. After the divorce, he had only agreed to leave after she had threatened to go to the police with evidence of the forgeries. The rest of her property then appeared to be safe.

Some months later, she began a very special friendship with a man she met at a party. His name was Eamonn, he was six feet six tall, and built like a tree trunk. He was a policeman. He loved his job and had always wanted to be a copper. She eventually got to know him so well that one day she told him all about the captain, and he, in turn, told her of all the things she could have done, or could still do, to see him behind bars. She was very comforted by his advice, but all she wanted right then was to feel Eamonn's weight on top of her. She adored big, heavy guys. She simply could not resist a hefty man with a strong, hairy chest, and broad shoulders and back, but perhaps most of all she loved the way he went so irresistibly soppy when she reached down between his hairy legs and tickled his balls.

One evening she was at home preparing his favourite meal of steak and kidney pudding. She had invited him to join her after his late shift, but looking up at the clock on the kitchen wall, she noticed he was a little bit late. She knew that a policeman's shift could be extended at very short notice, but if he was going to be too late he would somehow let her know.

Then, there was a knock at the door.

"Ah, Eamonn," she called out, relieved, as she ran to the door, but on opening the door, standing there was not the powerful and protective frame of Eamonn. It was the captain.

"You bitch," he hissed at her as he lunged forward, grabbing her by the neck with both hands. "You've ruined me, and now you're going to pay."

He pushed her further indoors, slammed the door behind him with his foot, then slapped her hard across the face knocking her to the floor. As he descended down upon her, she tried to kick out at him but he caught her foot and viciously twisted it. He kicked her in the side as she screamed, then dropped down on top of her and grabbed her by the throat again.

Then mercifully came another knock on the door.

"Help!" Alison screamed, hoping to God that, this time, it would be Eamonn.

It took just one good shoulder barge from the eighteen stone policeman before the door's hinges cracked and it crashed open. In a second, Eamonn was upon the captain who suddenly realised that his whole body was first rising, and then flying across the hall, quite smoothly actually, until he crashed painfully into the banisters. When Eamonn strode toward him again, Alison remembered thinking how weak and feeble the captain looked compared to this magnificent man still dressed in his splendid uniform.

"It's my ex-husband," she croaked.

"You're under arrest," Eamonn told the captain. "For attempted murder , and..." Eamonn looked towards Alison who managed a smile and a nod, "... and forgery."

He then advised the captain of his rights and asked him if he understood what had been said to him, and if he wanted to say anything. Again Eamonn looked at Alison. The captain did say something but the policeman could not honestly remember what it had been, so later on, in his pocket notebook, at the end of the entry for reply to caution, he pencilled in: No reply to caution.

Eamonn was back on duty, though, and by the time he had, for the second time that evening, returned from the police station, the steak and kidney pudding was in ruins. They just lay down together on the settee and, in each other's arms, went to sleep.

The next evening that they arranged dinner together, Eamonn took her out to a fabulous restaurant and, over a candle-lit dinner, he proposed to her. She accepted. She was practically bursting with happiness and soon after that the wedding date was set.

A week before the wedding, though, the worst possible nightmare came true. Eamonn was working nights, when he, and a colleague, chased after four young joyriders in a high-speed pursuit along a motorway. After reaching speeds of nearly 130 miles per hour, the car began to slow down and pulled onto the hard shoulder. At first it looked as though the louts were going to give themselves up. The car stopped, and the police car stopped behind them. The two policemen got out, but when they approached the stolen vehicle, one of the occupants jumped out and levelled a pistol at Eamonn's chest. Both cops dived for cover as the gun went off. The young man who fired the gun jumped back into the car as it began to drive off again, but when Eamonn's colleague began running back to their vehicle, he saw the big man still lying on the ground, face down, in a pool of blood. Somehow the other policeman knew Eamonn was dead, but with tears welling up in his eyes he managed to radio for an ambulance.

Alison had to give up work. Such was the depth of her grief that she had to have counselling. She attempted to commit suicide twice — once from an overdose, but she herself had telephoned for an ambulance reporting what she had done, and was rushed to hospital where she received all the necessary attention. The second time she tried to kill herself in her garage with the exhaust fumes from her car, and she would have succeeded then if it had not been for an inquisitive neighbour.

She had been receiving psychiatric treatment for a further six months until it was agreed that she was well enough to return to work.

And now, she had been back at school teaching the ten-to-eleven-year-olds for about a week, but every now and again, she would hear a piece of music, or see something, or smell something, which would remind her of Eamonn, and it would make her cry.

Quite early that morning, long before she was normally due to rise, she had received a telephone call from the farm. It was Jenny, the girl who looked after the horses.

"Sorry to bother you, Alison," she said. "It's Barley, he's ill, he won't eat and he's making horrible grunting sounds. I've called the vet and he's on his way."

"I'm on my way, too."

She got up, worried, wandering what could possibly be wrong with Barley, her favourite horse. Just fourteen years old he had never been any bother at all, but alas, when she arrived at the farm, the vet was already in attendance, and the news was that Barley had died. The vet stood there talking about kidneys, and infections, and blood, but she wasn't really listening. It was the last straw. She collapsed, sobbing.

It was one thing after another, but then, somehow, she found herself sitting in her car, in the school car park, just outside the school's main entrance, at ten minutes to nine.

Suddenly, she somehow pulled herself together, got out of her car and marched towards the main entrance. She strode firmly along the corridor saying "Good morning" to two or three other teachers, then walked right into her classroom where the majority of her pupils were already waiting for her.

"Right, class," she began.

"Good morning Miss Bunning," came a chorus of voices.

"Of course, good morning," she smiled. "Now, I want you to get out your writing books, and we're going to write some poetry."

Soft murmur of disapproval from the class.

"Come on now," Alison told them. "Co-operate please."

"There was an old boy called Buck..." began a boy from the back of the class.

"No," Alison said, firmly. "I want you to really put your minds to this and write a poem entitled Loneliness."

There followed a short period of general shuffling about, and Alison stood patiently waiting with her arms folded while many of the children searched for their pencils and writing books. Then she sat at her desk looking round at all the young faces straining with the effort of choosing words. Some were sucking their pencils, others looking round the class to see if any of their friends were already writing something. Some were just busily writing. Her own thoughts began to drift. Over the last ten years, she had been promised so much, but ended up with very little. Some would think that because she was from a rich family, she should automatically be happy.

After what seemed like three minutes, but was in fact over half an hour, she heard a voice next to her.

"Please, Miss, I've finished."

She looked into the young boy's face, smiled, then looked at the verses he had written in his book. At the top was written: Loneliness by Nigel Joseph, aged ten and a half. Alison read it, then with tears welling up in her eyes, she read it again, more slowly.

"That's beautiful, Nigel," she whispered. "That's really beautiful. May I read it out?"

"Yeah, okay." Nigel smiled shyly.

Then, pulling herself together she stood up.

"Class," she said. "Nigel has finished. I will read this out. It's very good."

After a suitable hush was established around the class, she began to read, slowly and quietly.

> I am not lonely, but I do wonder what it's like,
> With no one to love you or tuck you in at night,
> A kiss when you're good, or a smack when you're bad,
> It's better to be punished than to have no Mum or Dad.
>
> I like playing games though I'm not very tall,
> But you feel left out if no one passes you the ball,
> And then afterwards nobody will talk about the game,
> 'Cos you're not one of them - you're lonely again.
>
> And I know a lady who's best friend died,
> Then she was lonely - so lonely that she cried,
> I wonder what its like, what will she do,
> And I'm afraid that there are others like her too.

Having read the verses to the children, she just stood there, in front of her class, still looking down at the boy's poem, but in a kind of trance. Most of the children understood that her mind was no longer in the classroom, and they knew of the terrible misfortune which she'd had to endure. Even at their young age they understood all of this and were exceedingly sympathetic. They very much liked their teacher and they began to glance uneasily around at each other wondering what to do about her in her present state as she continued to stand perfectly still staring down at Nigel's book.

"Are you okay, Miss?" ventured one little girl from the back.

No answer. The other children started to fidget uncomfortably in their seats.

"Would you like to sit down?"

The boy who was still standing next to her actually took her by the hand, led her to her seat behind her desk, and gently sat her down. He then took his writing book from her, smiled reassuringly at his classmates and started back towards his seat.

"Yes, thank you," she murmured. "That was very good. One day I shall read it out to the class."

"But Miss, you just did," said one of the other lads.

Three girls sitting in the middle of the room gestured to him crossly, and in unison made loud shooshing noises.

"What?" Alison continued to murmur, and most of the children at the front of the class now noticed that she had tears streaming down her face, and the expression thereon was vacant. "What? Class? It's not like you to be insubordinate. Debbie? Jodie? Rick? What is the matter with you? I trust none of you is suffering from dysphoria. If not you will kindly tell me the meaning of..."

"Miss," continued the same lad, "not meaning to be rude or anything but..."

"Quiet!" she snapped, but then, in more measured tones, she said: "Now, who can give me the difference in the meanings of the words aphasia and aphonia?"

Absolutely no response.

"Right." Alison Bunning suddenly stood up, took out her hanky and dried her tears. "What we must polish up today is our Italian, otherwise none of us has a hope of passing our advanced certificate and you can wave goodbye to university."

The ten and eleven year-old children gazed around at each other in wonder. Then Debbie Joyce, the eldest girl in the class, got up slowly and went to the door.

"Where do you think you are going?" Alison snapped at her in such a tone, and began to stride towards her in such a fashion, that all the children now realised that there was something dreadfully wrong with their teacher.

"I have to go to the headmistress," said Debbie, and thinking quickly, she added: "You did tell me, Miss, that at this hour precisely I was to see the headmistress."

"Yes, I know, of course I did," Alison barked back at her. "And the reason is that Mrs Carpenter does not like being kept waiting. Did you think I wouldn't remember? Now hurry, child, or you will be late."

"Yes, Miss."

Debbie dashed from the classroom.

"Now before we continue," Alison smiled patiently, "has anyone else got to go anywhere?"

No answer, save for a few more uneasy glances from one child to another around the classroom.

"Good, then we will continue with our German. Rick, you will stand up."

The lad stood up.

"Is this German or Italian?" he whispered to the boy next to him.

"Or perhaps it's Japanese." The other boy grinned, only to be glared at by two very cross-looking girls sitting in front of him.

"Now," Alison said, oblivious to the confused mood of the class. "if I said to you, Guten tag, meine guten freund, and it was late on in the afternoon, what would be the politest thing to say, assuming of course that you were from the same social circles as myself, and neither you, nor I, were a tourist?"

"Er," Rick stood there, not daring to smile. "I thought we were doing Italian, Miss."

"Why?" Alison said sharply. "Does this class do Italian?"

"No, but you said..."

"Is it getting hot in here?" Alison said as if suddenly in a trance again. "Or is it me?"

"Open one of the windows," said one of the girls.

Alison stood there with her hands to her face.

"Yes, that's an excellent idea," she mumbled. "Open all of the windows."

As it looked as though Alison might collapse, two of the children took her by the arms and began to lead her back to her chair. Some of the other children opened the windows.

"I'm afraid, children," said the teacher, "that I have made a mistake. Now what I meant to do was .. "

There was a sudden scream from the back of the class, then sheer pandemonium broke out. Alison and the children at the front of the class, looked at the screaming group of children at the back, but could not quite take in what they saw. Loads of horrible, frog-like creatures were hopping all over the place. Some had jumped onto the backs of children and were gnawing at their necks, because these vile frogs appeared to have teeth, and snouts - *like rats*. Some of the animals were sitting on the window sills, and as they hopped in, they were replaced by more of the vermin.

"Close the windows!" shouted Alison, as she flew to assist the children who were being attacked.

As the teacher burst into action, tearing bodies of vile-smelling, evil-looking creatures away from some of her beloved children, her normal senses which she had taken leave of over the previous ten minutes, began to come back to her, and she found herself locked into this nightmarish battle. She hardly really knew what was going on, except that she had heard something on the news about these creatures which were like a cross between a frog and a rat and, somehow here they were. Anyway, her normal, quick-thinking brain was back in gear.

"Everybody to the gymnasium!" she roared over the dissonant din of croaking and squeaking of the frograts, and incessant screaming from the children.

"But Miss, we..."

"Just do as I say!" she screamed, tearing a horrid creature from a boy's hair. The boy yelled as it held on with its teeth, but then it let go, and suddenly started snapping and hissing at her, biting at her hands, twisting its neck this way and that in an attempt at a better purchase. She squeezed harder and harder until it squeaked its last.

Then it became still, but she held on, squeezing tighter.

Then it burst like a balloon full of green, oozing entrails which showered over her and the boy. Alison quickly decided that there was now no point in continuing to vociferate, so she just gripped the boy by the hand and ran out of the classroom. Looking back she saw the frograts hopping all over the place, but fortunately the other children appeared to have escaped out into the corridor, and the doorway to the gymnasium wasn't too far to run. She slammed the classroom door behind her and made her way up the corridor.

And there, the children were able to climb high up onto the climbing frames which were nearly twenty feet high. Alison had no idea how high these putrid frograts could leap, but she was damn sure that it could not be that high. She then ran around the school, with the idea of warning the children in the other classes, and getting them to join her class in the safety of the gymnasium until help was at hand. Running back down the corridor, though, she bumped straight into the headmistress, Mrs Carpenter, and Debbie Joyce.

"Mrs Carpenter," she panted. "Thank God! Look, its those frog things, you know, the ones on the telly. The frograts."

"Now, now," said Mrs Carpenter, holding up her hands in a calming gesture. "Everything's going to be just fine. You just need to come this way and have a little lie down."

"No, no, no!" Alison shook her head, exasperated. "You don't understand. I'm fine, but I'm worried about the children."

Mrs Carpenter gestured to Debbie. "You may go back to your class. I'll call Mrs Dixon to take over."

"No!" Alison pleaded. "You can't let her go back into that room. You don't know what you're doing. You're crazy!"

But Debbie had already turned on her heel and was on her way back to the classroom.

"I assure you," smiled Mrs Carpenter, "there are no problems in that room."

"Yes there are!" Alison bellowed at her, as she moved towards the classroom. "It's full of those horrible monsters."

"No." Mrs Carpenter grabbed her by the arm. "Now..."

Then there was the most sickening, blood-curdling scream from the classroom.

"Debbie!" Alison shouted, starting to run. She and the principal arrived to see Debbie Joyce spinning around trying to beat off about a dozen of the creatures which had set on her immediately she had opened the classroom door. One of the monsters was chewing at the girl's left earlobe.

"Oh, my Lord!" was all Mrs Carpenter could say as Alison proceeded to tear the animals away from the stricken girl. Mrs Carpenter soon began to help by kicking some of the frog beasts that were on the floor. Between them they soon got Debbie back out of the classroom, and slammed the door tightly shut. They quickly examined the girl to find she had several bites around her neck.

"All the children who got bitten will need immediate medical attention," Alison told the Head with considerable aplomb.

"Oh, Alison," said the Head. "I'm so sorry. I thought you were..."

"Listen, you daft old bag," Alison said abruptly. "You will now help me round up the rest of the school, and get the children into the safety of the gymnasium until the authorities can come and tidy up this mess."

"Whatever you say."

Mrs Carpenter rushed off.

Alison watched her go and nodded in satisfaction.

Debbie grinned at her teacher's way of talking to the Head, but she was also mindful of the other comments made about medical attention.

She knew that she, along with anyone else who got bitten, would need immediate help or they would surely suffer severe problems later on.

As for Alison, as she rushed around the school, helping, guiding and leading the children, she at last began to feel better. She was happy that she, at least, was back again and doing a good job. It had been fortuitous for the children that she had returned, and she had been with them on that day.

Chapter Eighteen

The sun shone brilliantly for the first time in more than two weeks. The grass was a vivid shade of green but the ground was still quite squashy due to the torrential rain over the previous few days.

John Farrell and Sue Sherringham walked quietly up the grassy slope. The view all around them was quite pleasant, and the hill, the garden and the fields all at once seemed to have acquired an iridescent glow. Hand in hand they talked softly to each other, one frequently looking affectionately toward the other. Now and again their glances would meet and they would gaze longingly into each other's eyes, then occasionally look down the slope towards the garden where the sound of childish laughter added to their enjoyment, and made them laugh, too.

John's daughter Sam was enjoying her sixth birthday party so much that she had hardly noticed that her daddy, and his new lady friend, had gone for a walk on their own, while John's brother George, and his wife, Liz, were taking charge of the dozen or so children and the organisation of the games.

At the moment they were playing Blind Man's Buff, and Sam was currently the one with the blindfold and was staggering around with her arms outstretched. George was watching closely to see that there were no accidents.

"Hey, she's cheating," laughed one little girl. "I think she can see?"

"No I can't!" Sam protested.

They were all laughing, and George's wife Liz went to have a closer look at Sam, but was sure she couldn't see.

"No, it's all right," she said, "carry on."

As they continued to play, John and Sue carried on with their walk further up the hill. After many minutes of enjoyable, relaxing conversation, she squeezed John's hand just a little bit tighter, then stopped walking. John slowly turned to her, put his arm gently round her and, for one heady moment, he was overcome by her pulchritude. Pulling her towards him, he had thought she wanted a kiss, but for once she pulled back slightly and went rigid.

"What's up?" John asked seriously.

"Did you ever think about getting married again?" Sue asked, looking deeply into his eyes, unblinking, as if trying to make out all the working bits behind them.

"I am the marrying kind of guy," he told her, still trying to move forward, but when she persisted in holding him at bay, he continued: "and I love women, I enjoy the company of a sensible, mature, and, if possible, beautiful girl, so yeah, why not?"

"And of course", Sue smiled, "she would have to fit in with your lifestyle, love children..."

She broke off and they both turned round and laughed as more children's laughter met them from the garden.

Then John said: "Of course the woman I married would have to love children, or at least one particular little girl."

"Sam," Sue smiled. "She's lovely - just like her dad."

"Thanks, you could tell Lou that if you ever meet her."

"She must have loved you once."

"Oh, thanks," John said, again laughing. "Sure, she married me for my looks, charisma, because I'm so sensitive - she said she loved that in a man, and..."

"And you married her for the same reasons, yes?"

"Money." John looked downward in mock shame.

"You're kidding me!"

Sue pushed him away, then gave him a stinging slap on the arm. John held out his arms towards her.

"Oh it just seemed the right thing to do at the time, but looking back we were never really made for each other."

"And now," Sue began slowly, taking his hand in hers again, "what would you, or could you, possibly do to make a second marriage work?"

"Nothing," John replied assertively. "Absolutely damn all."

"Oh," Sue huffed with an expression of disappointment. "Sounds like you've really put some thought into this."

"I have," John smiled. "No really, look, I've learnt one thing and that is if two people are compatible, they should not have to work their guts out to make it work between them. Their life together, whether they get married or just live together, should be totally blissful and should come naturally. It should be like heaven on earth - not a marriage counsellor in sight."

"So you think we should never argue?"

"We?" John was smiling broadly now. "You and me? Us?"

"Well, I mean," Sue giggled uncontrollably. "What I actually meant to say was, you and whoever. The point is, would you and this mystery person never squabble?"

John put his arms around her and held her tightly to him.

"I'm not quite saying that, but..." he pulled away now and looked very deeply into her eyes. She was, in fact, the most beautiful girl he had ever seen. "I'm looking for a girl, a woman, to share my life with, one who makes me feel comfortable, relaxed, one who easily makes me laugh, comforts me when I'm not feeling so good, has all those charming little feminine gestures like a sexy smile and a wink when she suggests something rather naughty, a woman who excites and takes my breath away, one whom I miss terribly all day long and I can't wait to be with her on my way home from work, and when I'm holding her she..."

He broke off as he suddenly sensed something that wasn't right.

"Go on," said Sue. "This is getting interesting."

But in the very next instant she noticed it too.

"The children!"

The sound was hysterical, but it was no longer that of childish laughter. Neither was it that of enjoyment and merriment. It was fear. Then they heard a cry of pain, more screaming from everybody, then George's authoritative shouts trying to control the situation.

"What's going on?" Sue turned to John.

"Sounds bad," John was already in full fight. "Come on!"

From the top of the hill they couldn't make out what was happening, but as they ran together, getting closer to the garden, they could see the children running, some were spinning as they ran as if afraid of what was behind them. Also, as they got closer, they could hear strange noises. Then John saw George - he'd got a spade from the shed and appeared to be spearing at something on the ground. Then, at last, John and Sue were at the garden gate, and what they saw made their mouths go dry, and their stomachs heave. Those creatures that they had both seen before, briefly, only this time there were dozens of them, hopping all over the garden, and chasing the children. The noise of croaking and squeaking was deafening. One little girl rushed past screaming with two of the vile, frog-like rodents attached to her long hair. Both John and Sue grabbed her together, and each took one of the creatures and began to squeeze. Sue's long fingernails came in useful as she dug them into the animal's grotesque body. She continued to squeeze, and the thing burst spraying blobs of smelly green and red innards all over the little girl and over herself. John continued to wrestle with the other hissing creature as it came off the girl still clutching a huge tuft of blonde hair.

"Help to get all the children indoors," John shouted to Sue, but she was already in action, joining forces with Liz who was kicking several of the creatures away from the little boys. The boys were holding on to each other, trembling on the grass. John could hardly think with dreadful cacophony of children's screams of fear and pain, coupled with high-pitched squeaks and croaks from the hellish rat-and-frog creatures. He still had the struggling, squealing animal in his hand. He threw it down as hard as he could. It lay there stunned, but before it could move again he stamped on it. He felt like vomiting when its insides squirted across the path. He hardly looked at its squashed body. He looked up. The women had got about four of the children into the house, but they were both out again trying to help more of the children. The nightmarish sight of the disgusting beasts hopping all around his garden continued, and Sue and Liz kicked out at them as hard as they could. Then John saw Sam. George was trying to help her as she had taken a tumble. She had only just managed to pull the blindfold off but now had at least six of the animals on her. He heard her scream.

"Daddy!"

John virtually flew across the garden. Two of the creatures were biting at her legs. John took both of them and tore their bodies in half before pulling them away from his child. George took one that was gnawing at the back of the child's neck. He held it on the ground, clutched the spade at the very root of the handle, then brought the cutting edge hard down onto the animal's head. It squealed for the last time, and its skull made the crunching sound of an eggshell being crushed.

Sue and Liz, who in the meantime had between them managed to get the rest of the children into the house, rushed to the rescue. As John struggled with one more of the repulsive rodent creatures, there were three more on Sam's back, then George, Liz and Sue took one each, but just as Sam began to struggle to her feet, Sue suddenly yelled: "Oh, John, look out!"

At exactly the same moment, two more, seemingly bigger than the rest, appeared from nowhere and launched a vicious attack, one biting into John's face, and the other onto his arm. John turned round in pain and surprise, then tripped over George who was still crouching in the grass. Sue quickly crushed the body of the creature she already had in her hands and, like the first one, with her fingernails it burst open with a splash of innards. She then dived over the mêlée of writhing human and animal bodies, and tore the snarling creature from John's face. She kicked it hard. It flew, then paused, stunned. It hopped back at her, but then George brought the spade heavily down on its back, killing it instantly. John was losing strength with the pain of the other monstrous creature still feeding on his left arm. Sue knelt down beside him, took the body in her hands, began to squeeze as tightly as she could, and John winced and turned away as he knew what was about to happen. As she'd done twice before, she managed to burst it. It sounded like the bursting of a balloon which had been filled with water.

"Come on!" George shouted. "Lets get in."

As he carried Sam, and the women helped John to his feet, they all looked around in time to see that the smaller creatures were hopping away, squeaking and croaking as they went, but the larger ones just sat there, still watching, but thankfully not attacking again. They all made their way back to the house where the other children were watching, terrified, through the windows.

Safely in the kitchen with the door closed, George was the first one to speak.

"What on earth are those monsters?"

Sue took a First Aid box and began dabbing at John's face with cotton wool.

"We've seen them before."

John grimaced at the stinging pain, but then touched Sue's hand and tried to smile. He then picked up Sam, sat her on the draining board and began inspecting her wounds. There was a deep gash on the back of her leg, and some scratches on her back and neck.

"We'd better call an ambulance," he said quietly. "Just to be on the safe side."

"What were those horrible things, Daddy?" Sam said, trying to control her sobbing.

"I don't know, my darling," John said, kissing his daughter, "but we'll have you checked out and you'll be just fine."

As Sue went to the telephone, John noticed that many of the other children were starting to cry, then remembered that some of them were also hurt. He turned to Liz.

"Check the other kids out so we can give the ambulance men an accurate report when they arrive. Here, take some First Aid."

Liz began tending to the other children, then Sue returned from the telephone.

"Ambulance will be here soon," she said.

George was curious.

"You just said you've seen these creatures before," he began quietly.

"Yeah, but we only saw a couple," John told him. "And they weren't as big. Then there was a report on TV and..."

"On TV?" George said. "I never saw that.

"Yes," Sue asserted, beginning to place some ointment on Sam's wounds. "We saw it on Morning TV News - in hospital."

"In hospital?" George said in wonder. "And what were you doing there?"

"Sue was in for observation," John told them.

George looked from one to the other seriously.

Then Sue chipped in and told George the whole story. She included how she had suffered a heart attack, and finished off with the report on the TV about the rat exterminators who had arrived on the scene where people had been attacked by the creatures in their own garden - the incident where the man, Baldric Smythe, had died.

"But then", John concluded, "those two rat catchers assured everyone that they knew what these animals were, there was no need to panic, everything was under control, and we shouldn't hear anything more about them."

"Famous last words," George commented dryly. "I think we should..."

He was suddenly interrupted as Liz's voice called from the lounge where all the children were now seated. "Hey, you guys out there. Come and look at this."

They went in.

"What's up, woman?" said George.

"I just turned on the TV to occupy the children, and then the news just came on. A special newsflash. Look."

There were reports on strange frog-like creatures attacking groups of people. Then a man being interviewed.

"That's him," John said. "Alan Brynn, and his mate Desmond Prickett."

"Yeah," Sue agreed. "They're the ones who said he knew all about these... frograts."

"Frograts?" Liz looked puzzled.

"That's what he's calling them - the frograts."

"As if they are his... own creation," John mumbled to himself. "I think it's about time I caught up with this pair of jokers, and found out what this is all about."

That evening, when they were on their own once more, the intimacy between John Farrell and Sue Sherringham continued, but now, possibly because it was so late and they were both too tired, John felt that the atmosphere had some sort of dreamy quality. Earlier on he had spent some time down at the hospital for tests to be carried out on himself, following the bites he had received on the face and arm from the frograts, but he had just been given some medication and told that he was just very lucky being so fit and healthy, and if he did feel any anxiety or fever coming on he should contact the hospital immediately. The consultant seemed to think that Sam and the other children would be okay, too.

Having checked one last time on Sam to see her fast asleep, he returned to the sitting room to find that Sue was sitting there on the settee wearing nothing but a pink, frilly, short nightdress, and with her feet tucked up under her bottom, leaning over onto a cushion in a half lying position, she did look extremely adorable and seductive. As he sat down next to her he also noticed that she had opened a bottle of wine and had pulled up the coffee table where she had placed two of his best champagne glasses.

"Ah, perfect," he smiled. "Shall I pour?"

She just smiled and made an appreciative murmuring noise as he poured some wine into the glasses. She was enjoying the comity which was developing between them. He passed her glass to her and they clinked their glasses together.

"Here's to us," he said as they each took a sip.

Then they placed their glasses back down onto the coffee table and then snuggled up to each other.

"You're so hot!" Sue said softly, gently unbuttoning his shirt, and when she placed her hand inside his shirt, she noticed how clammy his chest felt, and the hairs thereon were moist with perspiration. "I can feel the heat of you on my body," she said with some concern. "Are you sure you're all right?"

"Just tired," he replied. "And it is sort of hot in here."

Sue did not actually agree with that, but as she continued to undress him, she hoped that this was because she was turning him on with the way she looked, and with the feel of her touch. She already knew how he wanted to be undressed by her. As she got down to unbuttoning his trousers, however, placing her hand gently down inside the front of his underwear, she was slightly disappointed to notice that there was no sign of a hardening.

John looked dreamily at her. She did look lovely, but for some reason, for once, he did not feel like making love. He felt tired and hot, and just felt like sleeping. He continued to cuddle up to her cosily, and despite the steadily increasing wave of drowsiness which was washing over him, he contentedly knew that he was now deeply in love with her, and he closed his eyes still enjoying the feeling of her soft, warm, little hands undressing him.

He grunted slightly when he felt her fingers touch his penis, and hoped that she would not be too disappointed to find that he, for once, was not ready. He smiled with relief when she took her hand away from that area, but was still glad that she continued to cuddle him, making soft, reassuring, comforting sounds at him. He knew that some girls would take it as a major insult if, after all their efforts to be sexy, they were met with a limp, flaccid prick on a man who just could not keep awake. But Sue wasn't like that. She was not some old dog who thought that sex was the only thing that mattered, and she understood that men, like women, sometimes simply did not feel like it. The difference was that a woman could still please her man even if she did not feel like it, but on the other hand she did not have erection problems or a premature ejaculation to worry about. A man, though, if he felt like it, could at least partly satisfy his woman by means of his fingers or tongue, although using these methods would mean that she would miss out on the ultimate delight of feeling his warm juices pumping into her. In any case, Sue and himself had already made love thus consummating their relationship, so it wasn't as if she would be worrying about his ability to manage it. Some men, he had heard, were just not able to get it up at all.

He felt himself drifting into sleep, and he could feel himself getting hotter and hotter. He felt a sort of stiffness and throbbing in his chest. The throbbing got gradually more intense, the heat became somewhat unbearable, and the throbbing spread to his arms and to his face until this, too, became utterly unbearable.

Then came absolutely horrible pain. Then agony. He was having trouble drawing breath, then he began to struggle when he found he couldn't breath at all.

He was petrified. He knew he was about to die.

But then, thankfully, the intensity of the pain began to recede, and then he saw a bright light, a tiny pin-prick at first, but it grew and grew, like a light at the end of a tunnel, beckoning him until he could barely resist moving towards it. He wanted to move towards it, but he couldn't. Fascinated by the light's sheer refulgence he struggled towards it but he was being held back. As though in slow motion, he looked to see what, or who, was holding him back. It was Sue, but she did not look beautiful anymore - she looked old, and grey, and haggard, but she was pleading with him not to go.

"Stay with me," she was sobbing. "Please don't go."

Then his vision began to get blurred and the throbbing pain in his chest started to return. He closed his eyes. He needed to rest. There was a strange sound which faded in and out like some tintinnabulation, and then he heard voices - not too loud, but urgent.

"Oxygen, quickly."

"It's ready. Hold the mask down for a moment."

"We will administer Streptokinase in the ambulance."

"No. Better do that now."

John was aware of his arms being pulled, and uncomfortable things being pushed into him. Then he heard Sue's voice again, still crying.

"Streptokinase? What does that mean?"

"It's a very strong drug to be administered immediately after a heart attack. It quickly clears the heart's arteries, and rapidly finds and flushes out the problem which caused the attack."

"Will he be all right? Oh, please say yes."

"Thought we'd lost him, love," came a kind man's voice. "But thanks to you, I think he's pulling through."

"Oh," said Sue, sobbing with relief now. "Thank you."

The medics then strapped Farrell securely to the stretcher, and carefully carried him out to the waiting ambulance.

Two days after the frograts' attack on the children's' party, Alan Brynn sat alone in his living room watching the television and waiting for more news. He had also been expecting a telephone call from one of the Pest Control authorities. A spokesman from one of these had interviewed him the day before concerning this new strain of vermin. Brynn had already let out of the bag that he knew what the frograts were and how to deal with them. He and his friend Desmond Prickett had also promised people that there was no need for alarm, but since making these promises two people had died, a school had been attacked, and a group of children had been injured by the creatures whilst playing in a garden. As he sat watching television he continuously smacked his clenched fists together. He knew that he was responsible for what was happening, but was terribly worried that this whole thing was now out of control.

There was a knock at the front door, and on opening the door he found Desmond Prickett standing there looking just as concerned and agitated.

"What the hell are we gonna do?"

"Come in," was all Alan could say as he turned back to the lounge. Des followed him then flopped himself down into an armchair opposite Alan's seat.

"I won't say this is all your fault," Des told him, "even though it is. I won't call you the biggest pratt I've ever known, or the most careless, stupid little bastard, even though you are, and you probably realise this by now, and of course I'll deliberately refrain from reminding you, that if it wasn't for you then at least two people that we know of would not be dead!"

"Thanks," Alan replied with a wry grin. "Of course, I don't expect an actual standing ovation, but at this point it's still a comfort to have a mate who could easily have said all those things about me, but just wouldn't because we're friends. The important thing is that we somehow, together, find our way out of this slight rut."

"You fucking stupid shit!" Des suddenly screamed as he jumped to his feet and began pacing around the room. "A slight rut? What the fuck are we going to do?"

After an uncomfortable pause, Alan said: "Look, there's something that drives these things away, and it's possible that enough of this something could kill them."

"Great," Des sighed. "What?"

"I don't know yet, but that's what I'm trying to discover."

Des looked at him as if he was about to launch some sort of physical attack.

"What are you blabbering about, idiot?"

"Come this way."

Alan suddenly left the room, then led the way out of the back door and down the garden path.

"Ah," said Des noticing Alan's new shed built on the same foundation of the one which burned down. "I like your new erection."

"Eh, pardon?"

"A new garden shed I see."

"For my new experiments," Alan smiled. "Now don't panic, but I was given a frograt which was caught during an attack yesterday, but I've got it well locked up, it won't escape and I've been running some experiments on it."

"What experiments exactly."

Alan unlocked the shed and led the way inside.

"Now, just watch," he told Des.

Des watched as Alan opened up a cage which contained what looked like an ordinary rat. Alan took the rat, then placed it in the cage which, Des saw, contained the now familiar, awesome, frograt.

"Just watch," Alan repeated.

Des watched as the ordinary rat placed itself squarely in the centre of the cage which was about three feet long, then turned its back on the putrid mutation squatting there in the corner. The frograt began to snarl horribly as it crept toward the bristly creature. Then, when it was only about six inches away, the strangest thing happened. First it started to snarl and drool even more aggressively, but then it suddenly froze and became rigid as though it was made of wood. Then it started backing away.

"What the...!" Des was mesmerised by the creature's bizarre behaviour.

"Can't explain it," Alan whispered, "but you could have sworn that the frograt was about to attack and kill the ordinary rat, but then it becomes scared and backs away. But we're not finished yet. Keep watching."

As the frograt continued to cower in the corner, the ordinary rat turned to face it. Then it crept slowly forward, stopped just inches away, then turned its back onto its former aggressor. The frograt then began to tremble and made a pitiful, high-pitched whining sound. At that point Alan reached into the cage, lifted out the ordinary rat with both hands, then placed it back into its own cage.

Des was just about to say something when there came the sound of a man's voice from outside. He opened the shed door and there, standing in Alan's garden was a tall, muscular-looking blond man.

"What do you want, mate?" Alan called.

"You Alan Brynn?" asked the blond man as he approached briskly.

"Yeah, and who are..."

He broke off as the man suddenly grabbed him by the throat and pinned him up against the shed door.

The man croaked at him. "My name is George Farrell, my brother's just been rushed to hospital where he's in intensive care, and you've got some explaining to do."

It was some time later that the three men were all sitting facing each other having a sombre kind of *pourparler* in Alan Brynn's lounge. Alan and Des had, between them, told George Farrell the whole story *ab initio*. Alan had preambled by openly admitting that the entire problem was his fault, and Des had filled in by telling him about the frograts in the Smythe's garden, and how they thought they had solved the problem. Alan finished off the account by telling him about their most recent discovery, that the ordinary rat had some quality to defend itself against the frograt, and even possibly to overpower it and kill it.

"Has to be some kind of smell," George concluded.

"You'll have to try to find out," Des told Alan, "but in the meantime I suggest that we go back to the scene of the most recent frograt attack, then begin a search to see if we can find their lair."

Chapter Nineteen

Peter Hargreaves woke up with a violent jolt, then lay motionless, groaning aloud, breathless, sweating. A brilliant ray of light from a chink in the curtain caught him full in the face. Opening his eyes he groaned again, then rolled over away from the glare.

Then came the memory of that terrible dream, the same one all over again, the one that always brought him back to sudden wakefulness. It came flooding back.

It was now nearly a week since he and his comrades had been shot down and he had been taken prisoner by the Nazis. He remembered the skipper ordering them all to bail out, but he had been stuck. Then someone was helping him and they jumped together. He could remember the explosions in the distance, but then...

His thoughts returned suddenly to his present situation. At first he thought the door to his cell was opening, but it was someone trying the door handle as if checking that it was locked. Then he heard footsteps receding in the corridor, and two men's voices arguing. He heard that the conversation was entirely in English, but greatly suspected that this was another one of his captors' devilish tricks.

"We need to find out more."

"I nearly had what I was looking for but you buggered it up."

"Listen, I've had enough. What you want takes too much time which we don't have. I say we just get rid of him."

"Another problem swept under the carpet."

Peter Hargreaves strained his ears to listen but heard no more as the two men continued down the corridor beyond earshot, or maybe they just passed through another doorway. His bewildered thoughts returned to his dreams. Having heard the two men's voices he began to remember the others - the interrogation.

"Why were you not in uniform?"

"I don't remember - I'm confused and tired."

"You are a spy."

"No, my uniform was with me in the aircraft. I left in a hurry and didn't have time to change. Then, when we were shot down, I..."

"We have a way with spies, so don't tell lies."

"All right, all right, you win, I am a spy. Now please let me sleep!"

No answer. Just laughter. Mad. Insane.

He knew that he had to get out of this place fast. Almost drunkenly he began to extricate himself from the hard bed, then moved over toward the door which he found had not been locked as he feared.

Opening the door, and dressed only in cotton pyjamas and sandals, he stealthily crept out into the long corridor, and, careful not to make a sound, began to make his way towards a set of double doors. Where this would lead he did not yet know, and on his way along the corridor he noticed that there was a single name - presumably of the 'patient' - printed on a label affixed to the door. He saw one called 'Fox' and for some reason he tried the handle of this door but found it to be locked. He began to wonder why this one was locked, whereas his had not been. He wondered - another trick perhaps?

Strangely, on reaching the double doors, he found them to be of the sliding kind, and they promptly opened for him automatically. Stepping through he found himself to be in yet another corridor, then from the first door on the left, with a label marked 'Dempsey', he heard familiar voices again.

"Tell us what we need to know, then we'll let you go."

No answer.

"Come on. I promise we'll let you go home."

Still no response.

"Stop messing us about," came an aggressive growl, and Hargreaves stared at the door in shock when he heard two loud thumps and a violent crash as if someone had fallen. Then he heard a yelp of pain almost childish or even animal-like. Christ, thought Hargreaves, they were beating up the poor man, and possibly a fellow British airman.

"And now, twenty more milligrams."

Another yelp. Hargreaves had heard enough. With an increasing choler which was providing him with extra stamina and gallantry, he rushed to the man's rescue. He tried the door handle - locked. Then, with all his weight and strength, he threw his shoulder against the door which crashed open so suddenly he was nearly sent sprawling into the room.

"Stop it!" he yelled. "That's enough."

The two men in coats stared round angrily at the interruption. Hargreaves stood with his mouth gaping open at what he saw. On the table, wide-eyed and shaking with fear, and being held down by the collar, was a young cocker spaniel maybe about six months old.

"Ah, Hargreaves," one of the men said, regaining his composure. "How nice of you to drop in."

The other man quickly reached for something under the table, then produced a mean-looking, snub-nosed pistol which he pointed at Hargreaves.

"What do we do now?" said the other man.

"Don't know," snapped the man with the gun. "Got to think."

The two men looked at each other, gestured toward the door, then without another word edged their way around the table, and out of the door. Then they were gone.

Hargreaves spun round and stared incredulously at the dog.

"Dempsey?" he whispered.

The dog still looked frightened, but then sensing that he and Hargreaves were on the same side, he opened his mouth into a doggy-like grin and wagged his tail.

Dempsey then jumped off the table, trotted over to the far wall, and tried reaching up to something hanging there. On his hind legs he managed to touch it, and it swung a little, but his efforts were curtailed when he fell over backwards. Hargreaves strode over to him and, from the wall, took the objects that he sought - two pairs of headphones. Hargreaves chuckled. Maybe the dog thought they were rubber toys to play with. They didn't seem to be any use anyway, they didn't have wires trailing from them and they were not connected to anything.

"Here you are," he laughed, handing the objects to the dog. "Good boy."

He laughed even more when he saw the dog putting his head down into one of the headsets while holding them down with his paws as if actually trying to put the things on.

"Here, let me help."

Hargreaves put the headphones on for the dog, then adjusted them so that the earpieces each rested on the dog's ears perfectly.

Dempsey then kicked the other headset towards Hargreaves, and suddenly barked as if issuing an urgent command.

"Stupid dog!"

Hargreaves began looking around him. He felt that he should be trying to work on a plan to get out of here, and not playing games with this strange dog. He walked around the room, searching for something he could use as a weapon. Dempsey followed him, kicking the headphones ahead of him all the time while still wearing his own headphones. Then he began whining.

Hargreaves looked at him, exasperated.

"Oh, all right, if only it will keep you quiet, and if it doesn't I'll use them as earmuffs anyway. That'll give me chance to think."

He put the headset on, then to his amazement, he heard a voice, and it seemed just like his own voice.

"Ah, at last," said the voice. "Thought I'd never do it."

"Who's that?" Hargreaves spun round, then ran round the room nearly tripping over Dempsey. "What do you want?"

Silence at first, then the dog attracted his attention by sitting up in a begging position. Hargreaves began to wonder if he was going mad. The dog's lips began to move as if trying to speak, then while the animal continued its unusual behaviour, he heard the voice again.

"Don't get excited, man," it told him. "Just think clearly, and I'll understand you."

'It's a dream,' Hargreaves thought. Either that, or his captors were playing yet another horrid trick on him.

"No, it's not a dream, or a trick," came the voice, apparently Dempsey speaking. "And I'm not on their side."

Hargreaves thought he was on the brink of cracking up. Being shot down had been such a terrible, traumatic ordeal, but here he was, a man of reasonably high intelligence, having a conversation with a dog of extremely advanced intelligence.

The voice chuckled.

"You're so kind," it said, "but do not underestimate yourself."

Hargreaves grabbed the table to steady himself.

"Who are you?"

"I'm Dempsey, but then you already know that, Hargreaves."

"Yes, of course, how stupid of me."

Dempsey laughed. "We've got to get out of this place fast."

"How do I know I can trust you?"

"Are you kidding me? Be serious won't you."

"But I've never..."

Hargreaves broke off when he heard footsteps in the corridor.

"Quickly," Dempsey said softly. "Get behind the door, I'll get their attention, then you clobber them."

There was no time for further discussion. The door was already opening and Hargreaves dived out of sight. As the man entered Dempsey suddenly rolled over and played dead with his legs in the air. Hargreaves held his breath when he saw that the man was carrying a gun.

"Oh, dear," the man said. "Poor little..."

Then he began to approach quickly when he saw that Dempsey was wearing the headphones, and was just crouching down next to the spaniel when an almighty kick from Hargreaves left shoe caught him on the side of the head. He had no time to recover before a fist crashed into the back of his neck, then the dead weight of the unconscious man nearly landed on top of Dempsey.

Hargreaves stood staring at what he had just done. The man was lying face down and hardly breathing.

Dempsey jumped to his feet. "Okay," he shouted. "Now let's get the hell out of here."

Satisfied that the soldier was rendered *hors de combat*, Hargreaves grabbed the man's gun, then together, he and Dempsey rushed to the door and out into the corridor.

Searching frantically for an exit, and mainly just following his nose, Dempsey rushed first this way, then that, and Hargreaves just raced after him breathlessly. Soon they came to a large oak door which was heavily bolted.

"Quickly!" yelled Dempsey.

But Hargreaves was already sliding open all the heavy bolts, but still the door would not budge.

"Stand back," he told Dempsey.

He stood about six feet away from the oak door, aimed the pistol at the heavy lock, then fired a shot which reverberated up and down the corridor. At last the big door swung open, and Hargreaves and Dempsey were outside and running across rough, open land. They were now completely out of breath but they did not stop until they were well clear of the building's grounds.

When they stopped, while desperately sucking in air, they stared around them. In the distance, as far as Hargreaves could see, all along the edge of one field was what looked like a row of trenches, just like those he remembered seeing in films about the First World War.

"You are absolutely right," Dempsey told him, and looking back they could see the building now a mile away, with at least that distance again along what seemed like a very rough road ahead.

"We appear to be right in the middle of a battlefield."

They wandered wearily along the road which was, in fact, little more than a dirt track, fit only for tractors, or possibly heavy armoured vehicles. The land was very hilly, and there were trees all around and, to give them extra cover should they require it, there seemed to be a light fog descending.

During the first part of their march they conversed very little, but Hargreaves soon became more curious. He looked at the smart little spaniel trotting along next to him.

"Who the hell are you? I know you're Dempsey, but how did you become the way you are?"

"It's a long story, man," Dempsey replied. "I'll tell you all about it when we've got time..."

"We appear to have plenty of time on our hands right now."

"Well okay. It all started as a simple experiment involving myself and a young spaniel called Fox."

"Fox," Hargreaves murmured. "That rings a bell."

"A name on a door perchance?"

"Yes, that's it. I saw..."

"If you'd opened that door," Dempsey said reproachfully, "you would have found me in there - well, not me exactly."

"The door was locked," Hargreaves explained.

"Hardly surprising really," Dempsey let out a sigh, but then suddenly appeared alert with tail and ears pricked up. "Did you hear something?"

"No," Hargreaves said as they both stopped walking and stood still to listen. At first all he could hear was the very gentle breeze blowing in the trees, but then from somewhere in the distance, chugging up the next hill, came the labouring sound of a lorry or some other type of heavy vehicle.

"Quick!" barked Dempsey. Hargreaves saw concern on the dog's face. "Hide, into the trees."

The pair of them hid, crouching down. Hargeaves took the brief opportunity to ensure that both his and Dempsey's earpieces were securely in place and would not fall off if it became necessary for them to run.

Dempsey looked at him. "Thanks."

Hargreaves grinned back, feeling sure that the dog had actually smiled at him.

Presently, the huge truck trundled passed them slowly rocking on its suspension over the rough, uneven terrain. They were just heaving a great sigh of relief when the truck ground to a halt.

"Why are they stopping?" Hargreaves gasped.

"How would I know?" Dempsey fidgeted uncomfortably. "I'm sure they never saw us, so let's just stay where we are."

From their safe hiding place, they saw a giant of a man of roughly six feet eight with a large ruddy face, climb from the vehicle's cabin.

"Shit!" the man was muttering crossly to himself. He went round to the back of the truck and opened up the sliding door. "Hey, Ross! We're lost."

As Hargreaves and Dempsey continued to lay low, they counted sixteen hefty men begin to climb out the back of the truck.

"May as well stretch our legs," one of them laughed. Many of them took the opportunity to relieve themselves in other ways - some just undid their flies where they stood and urinated on the ground causing several steaming puddles.

"Disgusting!" Dempsey muttered.

"I'm surprised at you," Hargreaves suppressed a chuckle. "You guys just cock your leg up wherever you please."

"Not me," Dempsey said indignantly. "May I remind you that what you're looking at is not really me."

Hargreaves was about to answer when a shout from one of the men made him divert his attention.

"Where in fuck's name is this place?"

"No idea," the driver replied. "But that bloody research centre can't be very far."

"It would be well hidden of course, stuck in the middle of nowhere for protection."

"Yeah," agreed another. "But we'll soon find it and smash up those laboratories."

"And beat up anyone who gets in our way," asserted the driver, laughing nastily. "Those cruel bastards will pay for what they've done."

As their conversation continued, Hargreaves and Dempsey exchanged glances.

"I've got it!" Dempsey glanced skywards. "They're members of the Animal Liberation Front."

"That's it. They're looking for some research centre."

"Are you thinking what I'm thinking?" Dempsey sniffed.

"You know what I'm thinking, and I know what you're thinking, so you know that I'm thinking that you're thinking what I'm thinking, so you should know that I am thinking what you are thinking."

Dempsey shook his head. "With all that sorted out, let us go and talk to those good people."

They emerged from the trees.

"Hello there, you guys," Hargreaves called out.

The seventeen hefty men looked round in surprise. The sight of a bearded man in his seventies, wearing pyjamas, with a pistol sticking out the belt of his pyjama trousers, and a small cocker spaniel, both of whom were wearing some sort of electronic headsets, did seem somewhat unusual to say the least.

"What the hell do you want?" the driver yelled.

"We heard... ouch, you idiot..." Hargreaves broke off as Dempsey bit him on the leg. Then he continued: "... that is I heard something about a research centre."

"And what were you doing hiding in the trees?"

"Well, we weren't actually hiding, you see we were out for a walk when my friend here, I mean my dog, he said he needed a tree."

"He said that did he?"

"Well, actually no," Hargreaves laughed uneasily. "He just ran off without saying a word, you know the way dogs do, so I naturally ran after him."

"And you brought the gun for protection."

"Eh..." Hargreaves looked at the gun.

"Get on with it, man," Dempsey hissed impatiently. "Get to the point!"

"Pardon?" said Hargreaves, looking at the dog, then realising his mistake for thinking aloud, re-addressed the soldiers. "Sorry, I thought he said something."

All the men roared with laughter.

"He's just a raving nutcase," one of them said.

"Most country folk are," commented another. "It's all those years spent away from realty.'

"Look, please," Hargreaves began again, "I know exactly where the research centre is. I just rescued this dog from there. They tried to keep me prisoner, but I got lucky and we escaped."

"And the gun?"

"I bashed one of the guys over the head, then I grabbed his gun, and we..."

"What, they're armed?"

Hargreaves looked from one to the other. "They sure are."

After a pause, the driver raised a fist into the air and gave out a decisive shout. "Right then, you show us where this hell hole is, and we've got enough explosives and guns to see off a whole fucking army."

"You're on," yelled Hargreaves.

As two of the men helped Dempsey and Hargreaves into the cabin, one of them inquired: "By the way, why are the two of you wearing headphones?"

"It's the result of a cruel experiment," Hargreaves explained. "He won't be parted from them now, as if his life depends on them, and he won't go with me unless I'm wearing the same."

"How very nasty," the driver growled, slamming his door." Are we gonna sort out these cruel bastards or what?"

The truck bounced along the rough dirt track, then all of a sudden, Hargreaves shouted and pointed excitedly.

"There it is, gentlemen, turn off here."

"But it's nothing but a field," the driver told him.

"Yeah, and a mile or so across the field and you'll see it."

"Okay, suppose it makes sense to hide a place like that out of the way. Glad we bumped into you guys, otherwise we would have never found the place."

Soon they were able to see the building. The driver stopped the truck with still about a quarter of a mile to go.

"We're probably on their security cameras," he said as he pulled on the handbrake.

Dempsey and Hargreaves got out and watched the men unload boxes of rifles and explosives.

"We don't know exactly where all the animals are," one commented. "I suppose we could just demolish the front of the building."

"Yeah, right," another replied. "And as soon as we know that no animals are in danger, we'll smash up the rest of the place."

Then all at once, the soldiers began to march towards the research centre. Hargreaves and Dempsey followed a little way behind, having to trot every now and again to keep within a reasonable distance. 'A formidable and purposeful army,' Hargreaves thought, grinning to himself. Then he whispered to Dempsey. "Hey, what are these guys going to do when they realise that this place is not an animal research centre?"

"What on earth are you talking about?" Dempsey's thoughts came over loud and clear in Hargreaves' earpieces. "That's exactly what it is!"

Assembled in the massive hall were nearly a hundred soldiers, all wearing shabby, faded, grey uniforms and armed to the teeth, some with machine-pistols, others with flame throwers. In front of them, standing on a proscenium, was Ian Newton and he addressed the men through a powerful pubic address system.

"Right men, this is it. Our informers let us know about the planned attack, thankfully in plenty of time, and now they are on their way, but they won't expect us to be ready. Our mind transference tests, unfortunately, will have to be shelved for the time being, but we are now in control of a new secret weapon."

Newton let that piece of information sink in for a while, and looked around the hall at some of the faces. There were no questions or interruptions so he continued.

"Gentlemen, I give you, the frograts."

He pushed a button on the floor and, behind the proscenium, a huge curtain began to rise, and this revealed a great glass case nearly the length of the stage and at least ten feet high. It was full of the grotesque creatures as reported recently on the television.

All the men, with looks of horror etched upon their features, began to creep nearer and nearer for a closer look. They saw that some of the creatures looked more like rats, that some of them looked more like frogs, some of them were attacking others, some were eating their remains, and some appeared to be mating while others were actually giving birth. And the newly born ones were growing and becoming as big as the others within seconds of being born. Everyone crowded around the stage and watched in amazed fascination for several minutes. During this time they watched the bizarre cycle dozens of times.

"Look!" shouted Newton, pointing to one particular newly born frograt. "Just watch that one there."

They all watched it. It grew and grew, then suddenly it attacked one of its brothers, and killed it, then almost instantly the dead one was torn apart and eaten by about a dozen others. But the newborn one moved away then began to mate with another one, then moved away again until it was attacked, killed, torn apart and eaten.

"Now watch its mate," Newton told them.

They all watched as, within two minutes, she was giving birth, and within seconds more, the babies were fully grown, and so the cycle continued.

"I don't know where these diabolical creatures originated from," Newton told them, "but they will be a powerful new weapon."

"How?" shouted a soldier from the back.

Newton paused as he, again, glanced round the hall.

"They are highly venomous. They are so..."

Suddenly there was an almighty explosion from the back of the hall and an entire wall seemed to cave in. There were showers of stone and fragments of bricks, then when all the dust had settled, several hefty soldiers came charging in, all firing guns in every direction.

"There they are!" yelled Newton. "Get 'em, men!"

Machine gun fire was exchanged. In the confines of the hall, large though it was, the noise was deafening. Several soldiers on both sides were killed instantly, then one soldier from the side of the Animal Liberation Organisation, noticed the huge glass case containing all those innocent creatures. From a distance he could not tell what they were, he just unbuckled a grenade from his belt, pulled out the pin, and lobbed the casing so that it landed to the corner of the stage.

"Dive for cover!" yelled Newton.

No one heard him. There was a deafening roar of an explosion followed by a shower of glass and blood. The surviving frograts then began to hop and run all over the place, squeaking and croaking as they went.

Many of the soldiers standing nearest the stage at the time of the blast were either killed outright, or were mortally wounded and were now lying in pools of their own blood and writhing around in agony. Machine gun fire continued to be exchanged with more soldiers being killed or blown to pieces by the second. Soon, there were only two humans left alive in the massive hall - Newton and the soldier who had thrown the grenade. Newton was lying a few feet away from the stage where he had landed before the grenade had gone off. The soldier strode up to him, withdrew a pistol from a holster at his hip and levelled the gun aiming at Newton's head.

"No, wait!" came a sudden shout from the back of the hall.

The soldier spun round, and there, having only just arrived, standing at the back of the hall and aiming his pistol at him, was the quite elderly-looking Peter Hargreaves, and standing next to him was Dempsey. Inexplicably, both were still wearing those headphones.

"Let him go," Hargreaves told him.

"No," the soldier said. "He's guilty. He must die like the others."

"There's been enough bloodshed," Hargreaves continued.

"But he's..."

The soldier broke off as the most extraordinary thing occurred. From the back of the stage, from behind the smashed up slivers of glass, a door opened and out jumped a tall, slim, dark-haired man. And he began to bark ferociously like a tormented dog.

"Who the hell's *that*?" yelled the soldier as he staggered backwards.

"Who is it?" Hargreaves said.

"Oh, shit!" Dempsey said. "It's me."

"You?"

"Get him," Dempsey told Hargreaves, "then I'll lead the way back to the lab and I'll give you instructions so that we can sort out this mess."

"But you're..."

"Do it!" growled Dempsey, "and for God's sake don't let that moron over there shoot him."

Hargreaves took the man who was barking by the arm and, led by the spaniel who called himself Dempsey, went off to the laboratory. As the soldier continued to stand there with his mouth gaping open and his pistol aimed at Newton's head, Newton himself began to jabber incoherently, but neither of the men noticed the horrible slurping sounds as the remaining frograts continued to feed off the dead soldiers.

Chapter Twenty

Liz Farrell raced through the town in her Ford Fiesta at nearly 70 mph, and she already had a police car hot on her tail with its blue cone flashing, but she was not stopping. Following John's sudden illness, her husband George had gone off in search of Alan Brynn to try and learn more about the origins of the frograts with a view to destroying them. Now, though, things seemed to be a whole lot worse than any of them had imagined. She had heard on the news that a group of army soldiers had attacked and partly destroyed one of the ground floor wards at the hospital, and when the police had arrived there was evidence of the frograts. Lots of dead ones had been discovered all over the place. There had been a tremendous explosion which had been a grenade going off, and soldiers, together with some hospital staff, had been killed. Coupled with the evidence that Alan Brynn had already provided on television, that the poison from the frograts could cause hallucinations and madness, the police were assuming that the army soldiers had, somehow, been affected by the venom. Either they had all been attacked and bitten, or they had eaten or drunk something which had been contaminated by the creatures' urine.

Through the town now, Liz took a hump-back bridge at nearly 80 mph, and the car momentarily left the ground before coming down with a resounding bang. She looked in her rear-view mirror at the police car which was flashing its lights and sounding its siren. It was gaining on her, but she kept going. She had no time to explain to the police now. She would have to talk to them when she got to her destination which was Alan Brynn's house.

George Farrell, Alan Brynn and Desmond Prickett climbed out of Des's van just outside John Farrell's country house. George led Alan and Des through the side gate and into the back garden.

"This is where the attack happened," he told them over his shoulder.

"How many you reckon?" asked Alan.

"Swarms of the little bastards, man. They seemed to be coming from everywhere at the same time."

Des peered up the grassy slope.

"Except from up there," George said, noticing Des's glance.

"How can you be sure?"

"John and his girlfriend, Sue, went for a walk immediately before the attack," George explained. "They came running down again when they heard the children screaming, but until then they hadn't seen anything unusual."

"Well," Alan sighed at last, "let's start in the opposite direction, then."

"Okay," George nodded. "That means walking across this muddy field. Let's split up so as to cover a larger area."

"Right!"

Individually, they began to trudge across the field which led away from the grassy hill.

As George Farrell squelched ankle deep in soft mud, he began thinking about all the things he would much rather be doing than searching for disgusting, rat-like mutations. He thought about his wife, Liz. He had only been married to her for about four months. She was a schoolteacher and had loads of marking to do that morning, and he didn't want to give her more worries. She was quite fond of his brother John, and understandably, was distressed when he had suddenly suffered a heart attack, yet relieved to hear that he had been with his girlfriend, Sue, at the time; she had realised what was happening and had known what to do until the ambulance men had arrived. Knowledge of first aid was an excellent thing, George concluded. Everyone should be taught it.

Liz heaved a sigh of relief when she finally arrived at Alan Brynn's house, and seeing George's car, a mauve Astra, parked outside, she parked next to it. She got out of her car, walked up the garden path, and found the side door open. She promptly discovered that no one was in, but at that same moment the police car which had been chasing her came to a screeching halt outside. The two police officers came rushing up the garden path, and she went to meet them.

As the two officers in blue approached her, one of them was getting something out of his pocket while the other one began talking.

"Good afternoon, Miss. We have been following you, and observing your speed and general driving techniques over the last two miles, and we have registered an average speed of 69 miles per hour, with a top speed of 83 miles per hour. During that distance, one mile was through a built up area where the speed limit is 30 mph, and the speed limit along this highway is..."

"Listen," she interrupted him, "I really am in a terrible hurry. My husband came here to meet those guys who know about the frograts. We had an attack the other day, then there was all this news on the telly, so he came here to meet those men... er, Brynn and Prickett... but now he may be in very real danger. He was trying to find out if..."

"Now, now, now," said one of the policemen while the other officer was busily scribbling with a pencil in his pocket notebook. "Your talking is like your driving. It's much to fast."

"There was an attack on the hospital," Liz said patiently, "it was on the TV, and these guys may be able to help."

"Let's just talk about one thing at a time," said the policemen who was writing notes. "Who lives in this house?"

"Mr Alan Brynn," Liz said, exasperated, and looking at her watch. "But don't ask me his date of birth."

"Now let's change our attitude, shall we?" said the first officer. "You say Alan Brynn was on television, so you sped over here as fast as you could, in order to say what?"

"Look, guys," Liz said, just managing to control her temper. "I know you're doing your jobs, but I need *urgently* to find out where my husband is."

Just then, they heard the sound of running feet coming up the garden path, and they all looked round to see a heavily built, but debonair and quite neatly dressed, man approaching them. Evidently, he was a bit of a quidnunc, but he was Brynn's next door neighbour, and the presence of the boys in blue had attracted his attention.

"Can I help?" he said. "I live next door."

"Thank God," Liz breathed. "I'm looking for my husband. He was with the man who lives here. That's his car there."

"I saw three men leaving in a large van," said the neighbour. "They seemed in a terrible hurry, and I heard them saying something about the scene of the latest attack."

"Christ," Liz said to herself. "Apart from the hospital which was on the news just now, that would have been John's back garden."

She just hoped that George was all right. She wished that she had not agreed to let him go alone to attempt to learn more about the frograts problem

"Right," said the policeman sucking his pencil. "We'll need you to give us a statement."

"I just did, didn't I?" said the smiling neighbour.

"We need to write it all down," the other policeman explained. "Let's go into the house. I'm sure Mr Brynn won't mind, seeing this is a result of his doings."

"No, you don't understand!" Liz yelled. "I've got to get to John Farrell's house now. My husband could be in very serious danger!"

"You let us take care of it," said the first policeman. "You give us all the details, including Farrell's address, and I'll radio through to Control, and we'll have an officer sent there."

After a pause, Liz let out a huge sigh.

"Okay," she agreed reluctantly.

"Good. Now in the meantime, let's go into the house and take some statements."

Liz went in and marched up the hallway where she guessed a downstairs bathroom would be.

"Excuse me," one of the policemen called after her. "Where do you think you're going?"

"To the bathroom if that's okay," Liz replied sweetly.

"If you're not going to help us with our inquiries, I'm going to nick you for speeding and reckless driving."

"What do you honestly think I'm going to do?" Liz laughed. "Climb through a tiny bathroom window and escape out onto the footpath?"

"Eh...?"

"In this dress? The very idea is absolutely preposterous."

"Okay but don't be long."

Liz found the bathroom, locked the door behind her, then turned to the sash window. With a satisfied smile to herself, she lifted the window open, hoisted up her sensible, knee length dress, and climbed through. After a little jump she was out, and running back towards her car. Within seconds she was speeding back up the road, still several seconds before the police officers realised what she had done, and were again in hot pursuit.

Still gathering speed, along a country road, there was now another police car tailing her. Obviously they had been radioed by the other guys, but still she dare not stop for fear of wasting too much time.

As she raced towards John Farrell's address, her mind went over the most recent events once again. It was quite horrific, moreover, the news had mentioned the sad story of Peter Hargreaves, the veteran from the Second World War. Apparently he had gone completely berserk. He had found a syringe and had reportedly been going around stabbing people with it. Then he had burst in on a private patient who had been receiving treatment, attacked and stabbed two middle-aged nurses, then forced the patient down on his hands and knees, and tied a chord from a dressing gown round his neck. Threatening him with the syringe, he had then bound up his hands and feet and beaten him up, but the police had thankfully arrived in the nick of time to save the hapless patient from being hanged from the ceiling.

George Farrell continued to trudge across the wet, muddy field. His thoughts, however, were suddenly interrupted when he heard a terrible scream. 'It has to be either Alan or Des,' he thought. He began to go back in the direction of the scream, then he heard Des's voice shouting. As he continued as fast as possible through the mud, he saw Des in the distance and he was calling Alan's name, but so far he could not hear any answering call.

After another minute or so, George met up with Des, and together they scanned the field but could not see any sign of Alan.

"Where the bloody hell...?" Des began, but then there came another blood curdling scream. It was most definitely Alan, and he was yelling for help.

Together, George and Des hurried along towards the sound of Alan's call, then George, who was running a few yards ahead of Des, felt the ground suddenly disappear from under him, and he fell headlong down a deep hole.

"Ah, fuck!" came Alan's voice. George realised he'd fallen right on top of him. As his eyes became accustomed to the gloom, he looked up to see that he and Alan were down a hole approximately ten feet deep but only about six feet wide. They were both quite deep in soft mud which had saved them from any injury through falling.

Then he heard Des's voice from above.

"Are you okay, you guys?"

"Yeah, sure," George replied. "Got any rope?"

"Some in the van."

"Be a good chap and get it so that we can..."

He broke off suddenly as Alan continued to scream and yelp horribly. Looking down he saw that Alan was threshing around with frograts all over him. They were over his arms, legs and face, biting and chewing flesh. George Farrell's eyes were even more used to the lack of light now, and he clearly saw that the creatures were pouring out of hole which must have been a tunnel exit.

"Fucking well get us out of here!" George yelled, as he began to kick at the filthy creatures on Alan's face.

"Are there some there?" Des inquired. "Have you found some?"

"Move it, you moron! They've found us. We're being eaten alive down here!"

Liz began to slow down and, looking out for the name of a road, she took the turning and sighed with relief when she finally arrived outside John's house. Seeing the Transit van which she correctly assumed was the van the three men had travelled in, she pulled up and stopped. She got out, looked around her, and was just about to run off into John's back yard when the two police cars arrived, and four officers came running over to her.

"What you've done," one of the police officers said breathlessly, "giving us the run-around, is..."

He was abruptly cut off as a man in his mid-thirties suddenly appeared from John Farrell's back garden, and dashed to the back of the parked Transit van.

"Oh, fuck me down," he was muttering. "Must get some rope. Quickly."

Liz raced over to him.

"What's the matter?" she demanded, grabbing hold of the man's shoulders and shaking him violently. "Where's George?"

"Who?" The man stared at her with wild eyes.

She clenched a fist which she pressed under the man's chin, and snarled: "Where the fuck's George Farrell?"

One of the police officers placed a hand on her arm.

"Excuse me, Miss," he said. "We hadn't finished our..."

"It's the frograts," the man suddenly blurted out. "We've found their lair and Alan and George are down this hole."

"What hole?"

Liz grabbed the man by the throat with one hand while, with the other, she grasped his testicles and began to squeeze - slowly.

"In the field," was the terrified reply. "And they're being eaten alive!"

After Des had dashed off to get some rope, George looked down and, in absolute horror, saw that Alan was totally covered in frograts, all squeaking, croaking and, now, slurping. He realised that Alan, because of his total lack of movement, must be dead. Pressing himself hard against the soft, muddy wall of the hole, it did not yet occur to him why these creatures from hell did not attack him. Once or twice, an extra large frograt which resembled a rat more than a frog did peer closely at him, and did actually approach him snarling viciously but then, inexplicably, it backed away, and continued in its share in the feeding from the already dead prey. Vaguely recalling being told about the experiment where the frograt would not attack a particular ordinary rat, George Farrell suddenly caught the stench rising to his nostrils more intensively than the smell from the frograts' grotesque meal, and then, all at once, he understood. He had shit himself, and the frograts did not like strong smells.

He could not believe it. He was so petrified that he had messed in his trousers, then he began to feel it all oozing down his legs. It was hot, smelly, sticky and quite nasty, but he was grateful for it because it had saved his life. It had kept the frograts at bay. That was it. It was the very strong smell of something that these creatures did not like.

Again, a large frograt approached him slowly and snarled at him for a moment, but this time, before it turned away, George Farrell put his hand down the back of his trousers, scooped a large amount of the excrement, then hurled it at the creature. It squealed in surprise and fright. It certainly did not like this substance being flung at it, and it darted back to the hole which obviously led to the creatures' lair.

His mind was already forming a plan. Moving them away to somewhere else was not a long term answer. First, the creatures would all need to be 'encouraged' to move to one place, then trapped, then poisoned or gassed or something, but could it be that simple?

"Take that, you bastards!" George laughed, then scooping more of his own excrement, began kicking it at the other animals which were now covering Alan's dead body. They quickly returned to their tunnel, not appreciating the evil-smelling muck which, for some reason they could not understand, was now raining heavily upon them.

After another couple of minutes, something hard and heavy hit him on the head, and at the same moment he heard Liz's voice calling.

"Are you all right, my sweet?"

"What are you doing here?" was his reply. "You foolish woman!" and, looking up, he saw Des, Liz, and four policemen peering down at him. Des was holding a strong length of rope. He grabbed hold of the noose which had hit him on the head, then knelt down and tied it around both hands of the bloodied corpse.

"Okay, pull!" George yelled, "but prepare yourself for a shock."

"Why?"

Des began heaving on the rope.

"It's Alan," George called up as the dead body began to rise. "He's not a pretty sight."

"Is he okay?"

George shook his head sadly, more to himself than to Des who couldn't see him properly. He then heard an anguished gasp from Des, and some astonished muttering amongst the policemen as Alan's body reached the top of the hole.

"Are you okay?" came another urgent wail from Liz.

"Yes, my sugar plum," George sighed.

Then after what seemed like many minutes the rope was thrown down again. He climbed up using his feet against the soft muddy walls as support, and when he finally emerged at the top, Liz collapsed on her knees next to him and cried with relief. The fact that Alan Brynn had been mauled to death and George did not have a scratch on him, to her at that moment, was just miraculous. Once he was clear of the muddy drop, Des's attention returned to his late friend.

"Can't say you didn't ask for it," George heard him saying. "But we'll sort these little critters out for you somehow."

George knelt down next to Des and placed his arm on his shoulder.
"That, my friend, is exactly what we're gonna do."
"But how?" Des sobbed. "These guys take no shit."
"That's what I'm counting on," George told him, as Liz joined in for a cuddle, "but I do need to look at that experiment that Brynn was doing with the frograt and the ordinary rat, then with the help of the police, I think we may be able to formulate a plan."

Two of the policemen went to sort out their reports and collect the necessary information concerning the death of Alan Brynn. Meanwhile, George, Des, Liz, and the other two officers returned to Brynn's home where there could be, at last, the denouement George hoped for, and they would soon confirm the truth about the one thing which could possibly be used as a vital weapon against the frograts.

It was hoped that the very strong smell of something, for example, gas, would be enough to control the direction of Alan Brynn's horrid creations but, George realised, it was being somewhat hopeful to imagine for one moment that a putrid stink would be sufficient to actually kill the creatures.

Depending on the proof, and the confirmation of George's theory which, hopefully, they would soon obtain, the idea would be that they might somehow trap the frograts, and attempt to direct them all into one area where they could then be dealt with. Exactly how they would be dealt with once trapped was yet to be seen.

They went to Brynn's shed, and began the same test as before, putting the frograt into a cage with an ordinary rat. Just as before, when it looked as though the aggressive frograt would attack and, surely kill, the ordinary rat, it started backing away and making pitiful, timid squeaks.

"Right, now," said George as he suddenly opened the cage door and took out the ordinary rat. He then turned the surprised creature over so that he and Des could examine it.

"That's it, then," Des sighed, as he saw the evidence oozing out of the rat's hind quarters.

"Now you guys know about this," George told the two policemen firmly, "we tell the council, and anyone else who will listen."

He placed the creature back into its own cage before he got too much of the animal's waste all over his hands.

"Using some kind of very repugnant smell, we may be able to get these creatures into an area where they can be dealt with quickly without risking the safety of any person, or other animal."

"I think I know how to do it," Des said gloomily, still thinking sadly about the loss of his best friend.

"How?" asked Liz.

"Poison," Des said. "Somewhere amongst Alan's notes there is a formula for a poison to kill the creatures. Most of the ordinary rat poisons were rendered harmless by an injection that he administered to the original female frograt."

"Will it be quick enough, though?" George said thoughtfully. "Don't forget we'll be trying to contain all the frograts in one area, and whatever we do then will have to be quick and sure."

"Burn the bastards," suggested one of the policemen.

All heads turned in his direction.

"Use flame throwers," continued the young officer. "Trap them so that none can escape, then a group of guys could just march in with flame throwers. Should be fun."

The other officer gave his young colleague a terrific smack on the back. "Well done," he said heartily. "Now, why didn't anyone else think of that?"

George turned to face the policemen.

"You know," he said, "it's very often the simplest ideas that are the best."

Liz flung her arms around her husband and they cuddled to celebrate the end of the frograts.

Chapter Twenty-One

George Farrell and Desmond Prickett stood there in their protective suits, and began to check each other over, making sure they were both secure and properly protected. They put on their white, protective helmets as the other men from the Pest Control Department approached them. In all there were fifteen men - they had parked their vans a few yards away. Some of them were pulling along two big cylinders with pipes attached, while others carried huge long, cylindrical shaped things on their shoulders. These had handles and triggers like large guns, and George correctly guessed that these were flame throwers.

"Hey, what's the plan?" George called, his voice muffled because of the helmet.

"We go to the hole where your friend was killed," one of the pest controllers told him. "We drive the little bastards out with the gas," he gestured to one of the huge cylinders on its trolley, "then as they come out we fry 'em with the flame throwers. Simple."

Des and George looked at each other and shrugged their shoulders. They had to admit, it did sound simple.

"What kind of gas?" Des asked.

"Just ordinary household gas," he was told. "The kind we do our cooking with."

They started their trek across the field towards the hole where Alan Brynn had met his untimely death. It all happened a lot quicker than any of them had imagined. No sooner had the men unravelled the hoses from the gas cylinders and turned the gas on, than the frograts began to pour out of the hole where Alan and George had fallen.

"Start the flame throwers!" yelled Des.

The flame throwers roared into action, and the pitiful squeaks that came from below, and the sickening cracking told them that they were getting the desired results. Unfortunately, none of the men had realised how these creatures had bred in such large numbers over such a short space of time.

George saw it first. From a distance, it looked like a huge shadow gradually moving away from them.

"Oh, no!" he shouted. "Look! The bastards had an escape route."

The flame throwers stopped as they all looked up to see hundreds of frograts hopping together at an incredible speed. And they were moving back towards the school where they had been once before.

"Shit!" said the head of Pest Control. Looking down the hole he saw no more evidence of frograts. The ones that were left were all on the move.

"Call the police! We'll need all the help we can get to evacuate that school."

Alison Bunning was taking her class for Environmental Studies when there came a knock at the door and in walked the head mistress, Mrs Carpenter. Alison looked up and smiled. They were back on talking terms now.

"Sorry to interrupt, Alison," she said quietly, "but I'm afraid we have a little problem."

"Oh?" Alison raised her eyebrows.

"Yes," Mrs Carpenter continued. "You know the incident the other day involving those toadrats, or frogmice, or whatever...?"

"Frograts," Alison smiled.

"Yes, well, I've just received an urgent call saying they're back and we may have to evacuate the school."

Alison quickly stood up and scanned the room to ensure that all the windows were shut. She was just about to say something when Mr Jobson, the janitor, crashed through the door.

"Please, someone help!" he shrieked.

"What?" Alison snapped at him.

"Look in the playground. It's horrible. *They're* horrible!"

Alison and Mrs Carpenter exchanged glances, then dashed to the window which looked directly out into the playground. The nightmarish sight that met them made them gasp in horror. Swarms of frograts. The children excitedly began to crowd around the windows, then screamed in fright.

"Now, now, children," Mrs Carpenter made her usual soothing gestures. "Just take it easy."

Alison turned to Mr Jobson.

"Go round the whole building making sure all the windows are secure."

"Right!"

The old janitor dashed off.

"What now?" Alison said to Mrs Carpenter.

"We're to sit tight until we receive instructions," Mrs Carpenter said. "The police will be here very soon."

"You wait here for a minute," Alison told her, as she briskly strode from the classroom. "I've got an idea."

"Where are you going?" Mrs Carpenter called after her.

"To the gymnasium," Alison shouted over her shoulder as she was already in full flight down the corridor.

George Farrell, Desmond Prickett, the pest controllers, and fifty or so police officers stood around the playground wondering what to do next. Voices on the police radios chatted urgently. The first idea was just to go ploughing into the playground with all the flame throwers firing in every direction, but the opportunity of having all the frograts together, squatting as they were in the playground, was too good to take chances. Many of course would be killed, but hundreds of others would simply disperse, and possibly wouldn't be seen until they attacked again. They had to be trapped first, then they could be destroyed at leisure, but where could they be trapped?

A police inspector and the head of Pest Control were just discussing this, and the question of when and how to evacuate the school, when there was a shout.

"Who's that?" demanded one of the police officers.

From across the playground came a female teacher, walking tentatively around the playground so as not to disturb the frograts.

The police inspector went to meet her.

"Taking a bit of a risk," he told her. "You should have stayed with the children. We were just discussing the evacuation."

"My name is Alison Bunning," she told him. "Now, who's in charge here?"

"I am," he told her. "I am Inspector Turner."

Alison looked into his eyes for a moment. She liked him. He was big, strong looking and friendly.

"What we need, is to trap these horrible creatures, whatever they are."

"I know," said the inspector. "But how?"

"In the gymnasium," Alison told him. "I have it all ready. On the other side of the playground, the big doors lead straight to the gymnasium. You just need to manoeuvre your men towards the creatures, so that the gymnasium is the only place to go."

First, the evacuation, orchestrated by Mrs Carpenter, began. The children, class by class, filed out and, in their lines, they were led by their own teachers round the back of the school, then all the way round until they were on the field, back on the other end of the playground where most of their parents were now anxiously waiting.

Alison stood there watching. Soon she was joined by Mrs Carpenter.

"Thank God for that!" she breathed. "At least the children are all safe now."

They continued to watch as police officers and pest controllers surrounded the playground, then when it seemed that the frograts were becoming restless and hopping around wondering what direction to go in, the men began to close in. Every now and again, a small group of frograts tried to break away, but they were swiftly brought under control again by just a small burst from a flame thrower.

George Farrell and Desmond Prickett were also watching, but there was little more that they could do now to assist. The matter was in the hands of the authorities who obviously knew what they were doing.

"Okay, men!" shouted the inspector. "Begin to move forward, towards the gymnasium."

And the men began to edge forward, and inch by inch they got nearer and nearer to where they would eventually trap the frograts. The loathsome creatures began to squeak and hiss irritably, realising that there was nowhere else to go. Some continued in an attempt to break away with a series of hops, as if realising that their time was nearly up, but they were again brought back in line with a sharp jet of flame.

All of a sudden, a small group of about a dozen frograts broke away and attacked two of the police officers. Screams and shouts followed, and colleagues rushed in, kicking and crushing the putrid creatures until several other officers just stood together kicking the remaining animals back, and a flame thrower was briefly brought into action. Another policeman called for the urgent delivery of a first aid kit.

At last, the frograts began to escape into the gymnasium. At first it was a slow process, but the first ones through started to squeak and croak excitedly at each other thinking they were free, and this attracted the others, and in the end they were clamouring around the entrances, and hopping over each other to get in. It was like a crazy game of leapfrog.

With the last one in, one of the gas cylinders was placed just inside one entrance, and switched on. The gas began to hiss loudly, then all the entrances were slammed shut and locked.

"That's it," the inspector shouted. "Well done, everybody."

The crowd of people - police officers, pest controllers, teachers, children and parents - all gathered round the gymnasium, peering inside in morbid fascination at the frograts.

The repulsive creatures went mad and began to throw themselves up against the windows. This alarmed many of the children, and even worried a lot of the men.

"Christ!" yelled a young copper. "We're in trouble if the glass breaks."

"Should be all right," Alison called out. "That reinforced glass has footballs kicked up against it all day long."

She looked at the inspector who smiled back at her.

"Thank you, Miss Bunning," he shouted above the continual banging noise.

"Oh, call me Alison, please," she grinned.

"Oooh," came a chorus from some of the children.

"Romance between a teacher and a policeman," said a particularly cheeky, ten year-old boy. "Film at eleven."

Everyone laughed but their laughter was short-lived. It became increasingly evident that although the creatures inside the gymnasium were going quite berserk, they were not showing signs of getting weaker, and they were definitely not dying. If anything they were getting stronger. The shrieking was growing in volume, they were leaping, practically flying, around the confines of the gymnasium, and some were managing to touch the ceiling which was nearly twenty feet in height. And the ones that were throwing themselves at the windows were doing so with gradually more force.

The chief of Pest Control approached the police inspector.

"That gas should be completely used up by now," he said. "We've got another cylinder, and I've got a small explosive device, so..."

"What are you suggesting?" said Inspector Turner.

"We fry 'em," said the pest controller. "We blow 'em up. It might destroy the gymnasium, but it may be the only way."

Inspector Turner cupped his hands round his mouth and shouted.

"Everybody back. Everyone back to the field."

One of the pest controllers in his protective suit and helmet, stood at one of the entrances to the gymnasium waiting for an opportunity to push the second gas cylinder in next to the first one, along with a timer and a small amount of napalm attached. Eventually, with most of the frograts occupying the opposite end of the gymnasium and still behaving madly, he turned on the gas, unfastened the door, opened it, pushed in the hissing gas cylinder, then threw in the block of napalm. The timer was set for one minute. He slammed the entrance door again in the nick of time as about twenty frograts threw themselves at the glass. With a sigh of relief he began jogging back in the direction of the field to the waiting crowd of people.

As he approached, for a reason he could not understand, there was an argument in progress. Some of the parents of the children seemed to be at odds with the teachers.

Mrs Carpenter and Alison Bunning stood watching from a distance as the pest control man was setting up the explosion.

One of the parents approached them.

"Excuse me," she began politely, "but would it not be best for us to take the children home now?"

"Well," Alison began, "at the moment we..."

"Not until we've taken the register," Mrs Carpenter said suddenly.

"What?" said the parent. "You mean to tell me that they're about to blow up half the school, and you have not taken the register?"

Alison looked at Mrs Carpenter in disbelief.

"Of course I have," Mrs Carpenter defended herself hotly. "But following a fire drill, or any other kind of evacuation, it is usually done again before anyone goes home."

"Or before the school is demolished."

The parent was furious, and with the noise of the argument, most of the other parents were now coming over to find out what it was all about, and joining in.

"Look, you parents are with your children now," one of the police officers contributed.

"Yes, but not all the children's parents are here," said one middle-aged father. "Some are still at work."

Mrs Carpenter looked at Alison for support. "I... I... We had better get it done quickly now."

The pest controller returned at a sprint having set up the explosion.

"About thirty seconds to go. Everyone keep your heads down."

Alison Bunning looked towards the gymnasium, and then saw a small figure emerging from the corner of the building. She recognised him immediately as Dan York, a five year old boy from the infant class.

"Twenty-five seconds," somebody yelled.

Alison set off at a sprint, back towards the gymnasium.

Inspector Turner was a few yards away where he had been talking to a few of the constables, when someone pointed and shouted excitedly.

"Where's she off to?"

The Inspector and the other officers stared in disbelief as Miss Bunning went running back in the direction of the gymnasium. Then someone else yelled.

"Look, there's a boy over there. A small boy."

The pest controller who had just set the explosion yelled, "That woman and boy will both be killed!"

Inspector Turner dashed off after her.

Breathlessly, Alison arrived back at the corner of the gymnasium and grabbed the small boy by the arm.

"Quickly!" she shouted, pulling him.

But he struggled against her.

"No," he said. "I want to see the funny animals."

With no time to explain, she picked him up and started to turn in order to run back to the field, but he continued to struggle, she lost her balance and fell awkwardly. She tried to get up but her ankle had twisted badly.

The boy just stood there staring at her.

"Run, run, run!" she screamed at him. "Run as fast as you can, or I'll tell your mother you've been very bad today."

The frograts were also screaming, and banging, but thankfully the boy started running in the direction of the field, then she heard a distant shout.

"Ten seconds. Get the hell out of it!"

Then she saw Inspector Turner running towards her. He grabbed her, picked her up, then started to run.

"Five seconds!" came the distant shout again.

As he ran with Alison Bunning cradled in his arms, he continued the countdown to himself.

"Four, three, two, one..."

He dived down onto the edge of the playground with his body completely over hers.

The explosion shook the ground and roared like a angry giant which was hell-bent on destroying everything. The flash of fight and the gust of hot air was followed by smouldering debris, fragments of glass, and a thick cloud of blue and black smoke.

Seconds later, Inspector Turner was still lying down on top of Alison Bunning. He looked down at her face. Her eyes were still squeezed shut, and her teeth gritted together.

"Are you okay, Miss?" he asked quietly.

Her face relaxed and she opened her eyes. She looked into his eyes, and they both smiled. Still he lay on top of her, and she began to laugh.

They got up together, brushing dust off their clothes, and he put his arm around her as she swayed around on one foot.

"Ah, my ankle," she groaned at last.

As crowds of people came running towards them, she held his arm tightly.

"Thanks," she whispered.

"All part of the service, Miss," he said cheerily.

"I told you to call me Alison," she laughed.

He stopped and held her in his arms.

"Inspector Turner at your service, Alison," he said. "Inspector *Eamonn* Turner."

Chapter Twenty-Two

A couple of days after the tumultuous occasion at the school, John Farrell was continuing to recover well. He had been slightly worried about Sam, but fortunately, following her own injuries, she had only suffered a slight fever which she was recovering from now, and she was currently spending a few days back with her mother.

He sat up in his hospital bed, let out a satisfied sigh, rested back on the mountain of cushions placed there by a particularly attractive nurse who had a sweet, Irish accent, then opened the first page of a magazine lent to him by the old man in the next bed. He gazed in dreamy appreciation at the first spread in the magazine - about a dozen or so photographs over four or five pages featuring a stunning young model called Maryanne. She could not have been more than seventeen or eighteen years old but she looked absolutely divine, and John could feel his heart, which had all but completely failed him less than three days earlier, quickening and, all of a sudden, it appeared to be a lot stronger. The pictures featured the cute, slightly chubby, curly haired blonde, in various states of undress and progressively, as the pages were turned, becoming less dressed with the pictures getting more explicit and close up until finally, on the fifth page, there she was in a full frontal close-up in the sexiest of poses, sitting in a garden, with her hands seductively placed on her upper thighs and her legs wide open. With her naughty bit partly shaved the lips of her young, pink vagina where well in view, and as John continued to gaze at these tantalising pictures, he felt stirrings from his lower regions, the first of these feelings that he had experienced in at least four days.

He suddenly sat up to attention, however, and quickly hid the magazine under his blankets, when he heard well-known footsteps across the ward floor.

"Sue!" he called out.

Sue sat on the bed, leaned forward, threw her arms around him and proceeded to shower his face with soft, warm kisses.

"Oh, John," she gasped. "I've been missing you so much."

John smiled. He was satisfied to hear these words, and very happy to see her now.

"But it's only been a few hours since you saw me last," he reminded her.

"I know," she began to laugh and cry at the same time. "But I was so lonely when I went to bed last night. I needed you so much."

She leaned forward, continued to kiss him repeatedly on the lips, and as he leaned back she lay on top of him. But then she noticed a strange, hard but bendy sort of quality to the top part of the bed sheets.

"What's this?" she cried out in alarm.

"Oh, it's nothing," John said. "A sort of cover they put on your sheets just in case you're sick in the night."

Sue put her hand down between the bedclothes, and despite John's half-hearted attempts to stop her, she eventually managed to pull out the latest copy of Mayfair.

"And what's this?"

She looked very serious. In fact, John thought, she seemed a bit cross, but he wasn't sure whether she really was serious, or if this was merely an act.

"Oh," John began to laugh. "Those guys. I wondered what they were up to. A couple of the other patients were over here while I was asleep, then I woke up and they went off laughing."

"You telling me you didn't know that it was there?"

"Er, well, I..."

As John continued to stutter he noticed that Sue was beginning to thumb through the magazine herself, and a very curious smile came across her lips.

"So you like this sort of thing?" she said softly.

"Well, it did make me begin to feel a lot better," John admitted. "But it isn't mine. It's his." John pointed at the old man in the bed next to his. The old boy was smiling in obvious great amusement.

"You haven't looked all the way through it yet?" Sue said.

"Well, no," John replied in wonder, not understanding her deep, and sudden, curiosity in a harmless glossy magazine.

Then Sue got up and gently placed the magazine back on the old man's bed.

"Will you autograph it?" said the old man. "I think you're really lovely."

"Remind me again before I leave," Sue smiled.

John looked at the old man, puzzled.

"What's all this?" he said in a demanding voice. "You know something I don't?"

"She's done an old man the power of good," the old man laughed. "You're a very lucky young man."

Sue sat there giggling to herself, but John could not help feeling somewhat perplexed. There was definitely some sort of secret between her and the old man and he could not guess for the life of him what it was all about. Sue sat down on his bed once again, and cuddled back up to him.

After quite a long pregnant pause, John quickly looked around him to see if there were any nurses in sight. He knew he had an auscultation coming up soon, and there was something he needed to sort out with Sue first.

"Sue," he said in a croaky voice, "There's been something I've been meaning to ask you."

"Oh?"

Sue pushed herself away from him slightly with a surprised sort of smile.

John held both her hands in his, and looked into her face thinking how beautiful she was.

"I know you're very young and you've often said that there are things that you would prefer to do before you settle down, well, a lot of those things are the sort of things that two people could do together, in fact the enjoyment of such things could be greatly increased by doing them with not just anybody, but someone you are very close to, someone who wants to be with you, someone you want to be with, someone who needs to..."

"Hello, there," came George and Liz's cheery voices in unison. "How's it going?"

"Yeah, okay," John replied with a weary smile as the two new visitors seated themselves down on bedside chairs.

"Well," said George, slapping the side of John's bed, "The nightmare is over."

"What nightmare?" said John and Sue together.

George throw up his arms in disbelief.

"The frograts," Liz explained. "They're all dead. Haven't you seen the news?"

"I heard about the explosion at the school," John murmured. "The creatures were trapped."

"That's it," George went on, "but the explosion was not part of the original plan, and had it not been for a very brave teacher, and an equally brave police inspector, the day could have ended in tragedy. Anyway, in the end the explosion did the trick. All the little critters were fried alive."

"Urgh," said Sue. "How utterly horribly disgusting."

After a long pause, John turned to Liz.

"Please could you take your husband for a walk somewhere for about ten minutes. I need to talk to Sue alone."

Sue looked at John in surprise. Liz winked at George and led him by the hand up the corridor towards the coffee machine.

Once they were out of sight, John turned back to Sue, held both of her soft little hands in his once again, and continued.

"Like I was saying, you should want to be with someone who needs you and loves you, and so..."

"Why?" Sue suddenly blurted out. "Don't you love me?"

"Of course I do," John said, confused. "And this was the exact reason that I was going to ask you to..."

John was cut off again, this time by a fat, middle-aged nurse who suddenly appeared from nowhere and pushed a thermometer into his mouth.

"Oh, bollocks!" he tried to say , but sounded so incoherent that neither she or Sue noticed. By the time the nurse had taken her thermometer out and disappeared, John could see George and Liz returning slowly from the other side of the ward.

"Quickly!" John hissed suddenly.

"What?" Sue laughed. "What on earth is the matter?"

"Just answer me this. Will you..."

"Answer me what?" Sue continued, as a woman typically would. While time was of the essence, asking more questions while the poor man was actually trying to ask her this difficult question.

"Will you marry me?" John let out an almighty, relieved breath. He had finally got there - even if the answer was no.

Sue sat there, mouth wide open in a huge smile, and she looked as though she was just on the verge of saying something.

Just then, though, John heard George's voice. He sounded, surprised for some reason. Amazed, even flabbergasted.

John looked round to see George at the foot of the old man's bed thumbing through the centre pages of *Mayfair*.

"I do not believe it!" George was saying. "These are fan-bloody-tastic."

John was sure that George then said under his breath: "John, you lucky son of a bitch."

Liz came and stood next to George, her mouth hung open, then George and Liz, at precisely the same moment, gazed up and directed their stares at Sue.

John looked at Sue whose face went bright red, but she smiled sweetly at John.

"They're for you," she told him. "Before you ended up in hospital, I wanted to give you a treat. A photographer saw me in the town one day and just asked me if I'd fancy doing a bit of modelling. I wanted to do it for you, but I never dreamed you'd find out like this."

John's mouth just opened and closed like a goldfish, then he mumbled: "How could you?"

Sue backed away slightly. "But you said only five minutes ago that it's the sort of thing that makes you feel better."

"Yes, but that was another girl," John countered hotly. "And you are supposed to be for my eyes only."

"So you can admire other girls but you don't want me to be admired by other men."

While they argued, still holding the magazine open at it's centre pages, George walked over to John's bed and lay the magazine down in front of John.

"Look," he said quietly.

John looked down, and there was the most beautiful picture of Sue, so professionally and tastefully photographed that he could not very well complain. She was totally naked, but lying down on her side, she had her legs together and she did not look at all vulgar. Just obviously proud of her femininity, and with a terrific air of confidence, she had one arm resting with her hand on the side of her thigh, and with her other elbow in front of her, her body was curved slightly with her chin resting delicately on the back of her other hand.

"Oh," John whispered, as he began to look at the other pictures on the preceding few pages which he found were just as tasteful, and every bit as beautiful. On the very last picture, at the bottom, there was a caption which read: 'For my darling boyfriend, John, I will love you forever'.

Now in a somewhat lachrymatory mood, John looked at Sue. The tears welling up in his eyes were partly in embarrassment but partly in happiness, and he had not experienced this kind of beautiful joy for a very long time. He realised how bloody lucky he was.

"I'm sorry," he managed to whisper. "You're beautiful and I'm a pratt."

"Steady now." came George's voice as he and Liz took their seats once again.

"Bastard!" John said under his breath.

But Sue, all of a sudden, got up and sat on George's lap, put her arms round his neck and gave him a huge, wet, smothering kiss. John and Liz starred in amazement.

"Bastard!" John hissed, this time not quite under his breath.

And finally, Sue stood up, returned to John sitting next to him on his bed, put her arms around him and pressed her cheek fondly into his. Then she said: "I thought it would be all right to kiss my future brother-in-law."

Epilogue

Beneath the old rotten fence which had been knocked flat during a storm over a year ago, by the rundown farmhouse, in the overgrown neglected garden, lurked the hideous living thing. For days it had been left alone and was becoming weak with hunger.

Instinct told it that the other creature was now dead.

Slowly it began to move towards the dead creature, bit into its soft belly and sucked in its innards, chewing and swallowing greedily.

Then it sniffed the air and began to follow the smell of water. All the time it was continuing to feel stronger and less than a mile away, by the river, concealed high up in a tree, were the two yellow tree frogs. They were beginning to get used to their new surroundings now and had, at last, after days of high-pitched communication, found each other.

Instinct would, from now onwards, keep them together

Epilogue - Part Two
(Six Months Later)

Having put her three children quietly to bed, Kirstie Harris sat herself down on her new sofa, plonked her steaming cup of cocoa down on her new coffee table, and in a comfortably lazy and relaxed, laid-back position, with her legs delicately crossed, she let out a big sigh.

There she sat in nothing but her short, black, lacy nightdress. Once the children were all in bed, and especially when there was nobody else around, she found nothing more relaxing than lounging around the house wearing only skimpy night clothes, or just her undies, or sometimes nothing at all.

She was happy now - happier than she had been for a long time. She had just received good news from the college that she had passed the first part of her course, and now, with Christmas just around the corner to look forward to, she was confident of doing well in the forthcoming year which would be vital for her plans in welfare and her work with the council.

She leaned forward, took a sip of cocoa, then leaned back again and began to read through some of the newsletters that she had received from the college. With a faint smile, she suddenly realised who one of her lecturers was going to be next term - none other than John Farrell.

For some weeks now she had been having some regrets over the way she had treated him. No wonder he had been so upset at the time. Okay, he had pulled a bit of a fast one on her, but he had been desperate to explain afterwards, and had insisted that he still loved her. She must have seemed a bit cold and nonchalant towards him considering everything he had done for her, and more than a little cruel and indifferent.

Then she read an article which John had written for the college newsletter, and she finally decided that she would put matters right as soon as possible. She picked up her telephone which was on the arm of her sofa, and tapped out the number which, even after all these months, she had not forgotten.

It was answered almost instantly - a young lady's voice.

"Oh, I'm sorry," she blurted out, having been taken completely off guard. She had not expected anyone else to answer. "Just a message for Mr Farrell. I'm a student from the college. Thank him very much. I've never had anything dedicated to me before. It was beautiful."

"You can speak to him personally," came the friendly, female voice. "No problem, he's right here."

"Oh, no," she was confused. Was this John's new girlfriend? "I don't wish to disturb him, I just..."

"Who shall I say is calling?"

'Oh, crikey,' she thought. She could not possibly give this woman her name.

"Tell him it's... it's..."

"Yes?"

"It's Kim."

"Okay, just a sec."

Then Kirstie hung up. She looked for a long time at her telephone as if expecting to see somebody coming out of it. She then replaced the receiver and sat back again.

She got up, walked to the window, and looked out into the dark, winter's night. Some mistakes, she knew, were difficult to bounce back from, but she was a determined young woman, and she decided that, one way or another, she would sort things out for herself. At that moment she realised what she wanted and she felt confident she would get her man.

Then, in the shadowy lamplight in her front garden, she thought she saw some movement - a sort of hopping thing like a frog, but as she concentrated and tried to focus more closely, she saw nothing. Only blackness.

"Couldn't have been a frog," she muttered to herself. "Not in this sort of weather." She soon forgot all about it.

And despite the chilly conditions outside, and the frost upon her lawn, she remained optimistic about a bright and happy future.

...To be continued.

Coming soon from the author of The Frograts...

The Mist

As they live and breathe, they excrete and perspire, and as they do so the surviving frograts exude a wispy vapour. As they multiply, the mist gets thicker and begins to spread across the woods, and it hangs along the river like a dense cloud. Some of the hideous frograts continue to live on land, while others take to the water. From the depth of the river lurk those odious frograts which have now developed gills. And from the trees come the tree frogs - highly poisonous, these are also growing in number. Soon, no human is safe near the river or woods. If the poisonous frogs don't get you, the frograts will.

Police Constable Marty Brolin is reluctantly placed in charge of investigating gory deaths by the river while endeavouring to sort out his own marital problems. Now his wife claims that he is not the father to their new baby. And gradually, all the while, The Mist is moving along the river towards the town.